JUDGEMENT DAY AT YUMA

JUDGEMENT DAY AT YUMA

by

Clayton Nash

Dales Large Print Books
Long Preston, North Yorkshire,
BD23 4ND, England.

British Library Cataloguing in Publication Data.

Nash, Clayton
   Judgement day at Yuma.

   A catalogue record of this book is
   available from the British Library

   ISBN   1-84262-138-6 pbk

First published in Great Britain 2001 by Robert Hale Ltd.

Cover illustration © FABA by arrangement with
Norma Editorial S.A.

The right of Keith James Hetherington to be identified as the
author of this work has been asserted by him in accordance with
the Copyright, Designs and Patents Act, 1988

Published in Large Print 2001 by arrangement with
Robert Hale Limited

Dales Large Print is an imprint of Library Magna Books Ltd.

Printed and bound in Great Britain by
T.J. (International) Ltd., Cornwall, PL28 8RW

1

Even Break

'Frank Dallas, by God!'

He was hunched over a pair of drinks, standing apart from the other customers, when he heard the name dropped into the low-level noise of the saloon bar.

What noise there was stopped abruptly.

He figured he had better show some reaction, so he looked up sharply and glanced around the smoke-hazed room, hoping his face showed mild bewilderment.

'Where?' he asked softly, thinking it would help declare his innocence.

'Hell, right where you're standin', mister!'

It was the same voice that had spoken his name a few seconds earlier. He identified the man in a small group halfway down the curving bar. Fairly young, arrogant set to his head, face flushed from drinking rotgut, crossed gunbelts with both holster bases rawhided to his thighs.

A man who figured he was pretty damn good with his six-guns – and itching to prove it.

A man on the prod – hunting glory.

'*That* old man's Dallas?' someone further along the bar spoke up.

'He ain't that old,' said the glory-hunter. 'That frontier moustache and the stubble make him look older'n he is. The long hair, too. But that's the way you want it, ain't it, Dallas?' The man leaned forward, a slight twist to his mouth now, a hardening of the voice. 'Don't want no one to recognize you. Just aimin' to sneak in here and down a coupla drinks, then fade away – hopin' no one'd pick you out. Then you wouldn't have to go for your gun and let everyone see how much you've slowed down.'

'Harve!' said the worried-looking barkeep. 'Take it easy, huh?'

'Oh, I aim to, Burt.' Harve didn't move his narrowed gaze from the man he had called Frank Dallas. ''Cause it *will* be easy downin' this has-been ... past your prime ain't you, Dallas?'

'Happens to all of us,' the man with the frontier moustache said, not admitting anything.

Harve curled a lip. 'Must be outa practice now. Ain't been heard of since that gunfight with Claw Seeton up in Utah – must be – what? Year ago now...?'

'One year – two months – fifteen days.'

The voice was calm, a mite weary, as the man pushed slowly off the bar.

The drinkers hurriedly moved back, gathered in a far corner of the room.

Except for Harve.

The sweating barkeep made one final try, leaning across the wet counter, forcing a grin. 'Say, gents, how about you sit down in comfort and talk about things over a bottle of my best bourbon? On the house...'

Harve didn't even look at the man, just

swung his right arm up and back, hard knuckles smacking Burt squarely on the nose. The man staggered back with a shocked grunt, one flailing arm knocking bottles and glasses flying from the counter top, his cupped hand under his nostrils starting to fill with blood.

'You bust my nose!' he gulped.

'Go wash up, barkeep,' the man called Dallas said, in that calm, tired voice. 'I can see there's no way around this with a snake like Harve. Met his kind before, a hundred times.' He flicked bullet-like grey eyes to Harve's half-smiling face. 'Got to end in gunsmoke, right?'

'*Damn* right!' Harve gritted, flexing his fingers, setting himself, feet spread. 'Any time you say, old man!'

'Might as well be now,' Dallas said easily, and his six-gun came up thundering, and Harve was blown back down the bar, hit the curve with his spine and arched before catapulting forward a few wobbly steps, and then spread out on his face on the filthy floor.

'Judas Priest!' a voice hissed from the stunned crowd. 'Harve ain't even got one gun clear of leather!'

Frank Dallas continued to stare down at the man he had just killed a moment longer, no remorse on his face, only a great weariness just showing beneath the hardness. He holstered his smoking gun, returned to his drinks, downed the remains of the redeye and emptied his beer glass.

No one else in the bar-room had moved. They were all staring at Dallas. He dug a silver dollar from his pocket, slapped it on the bar in front of the barkeep who was holding a blood-spotted towel to his face now.

'Pine headboard ought to be good enough for the likes of Harve,' Dallas said and turned away.

'He won't be missed around here.' Burt's voice was muffled. 'He's been in a lotta trouble–'

He broke off, looking past Dallas who had stopped now, staring at the batwings.

A big man stood there between the slatted flaps, silhouetted against the street's sunlight, a double-barrelled Greener held at the ready. Dallas couldn't see his face, which was in shadow, but he saw the head turn in his direction. The Greener's barrels moved upwards slightly and the big man came forward.

Dallas sighed when he saw the tin star pinned to the man's shirt pocket.

'Sheriff Lake – you're who?'

Dallas didn't answer, watching the lawman's approach warily. His hands hadn't moved from down at his side but the right one was touching the leather of his holster.

When he didn't answer, someone in the crowd said, a little hoarsely, 'He's Frank Dallas, Arch!'

Big Arch Lake stopped a yard in front of Dallas, between him and the batwings. 'An' you just downed Harve Lester.'

Dallas didn't deny or confirm.

'Never seen nothin' like it, Arch!' the bloody-faced barkeep said, stepping for-

12

ward. 'Harve pushed it as usual...'

'Harve never even got his guns clear of leather!' someone said with a touch of indignation.

Lake's eyes narrowed. He was a man in his prime, looked healthy and felt it, and he wouldn't take sass from anybody. 'You a mite quick on the trigger, mebbe, Dallas?'

'I haven't said my name's Dallas.'

'It is, though. Recognize you now from a coupla wanted dodgers. One for Prado, Utah, 'nother for Carson City, Nevada.'

'Nothing in those for you, Sheriff. They were sorted out long ago.'

Lake almost smiled. 'You're admittin' to bein' Dallas.'

The man said nothing.

'Yeah, I know your name ain't on any wanted dodger I got right now... So, you took on poor ol' Harve. Now you're in more trouble than you can shake a stick at.'

Dallas arched brown eyebrows. 'How so? He called me. It was fair and square.' He gestured to the room, saying *ask anyone here.*

Before the lawman could speak, the man who had claimed Harve hadn't had time to clear his guns from leather stepped out of the crowd – average height and looks, a cowboy by his clothes.

'Harve meant nothin' to me, Arch. You know we'd tangled plenty of times. Hell, Harve tangled with *everyone* sooner or later.'

'Only once with me,' Lake said heavily, and the cowboy nodded.

'Yeah – well, it's right he prodded this Dallas into it, busted Burt's nose for good measure, but – well, I like to see *anyone* get a fair shake, an' I gotta say it din' look like Harve got that this time.' He turned to the others. 'Anyone else back me?'

'Hell, who cares? Harve was a mean son of a bitch who had folk in this town buffaloed. You might not think so, Arch, but Harve did just about what he liked, and scared folk white, threatening to kill 'em or their families if they reported him.'

Lake glared at the speaker. 'Shut your mouth, Cable! I run a tight town here! Me and the judge!'

'You run it the way you want!' a voice said, and there was movement in the middle of the crowd as someone ducked for cover.

The sheriff looked flushed, the Greener swinging a little indiscriminately now, making the men uneasy. He rested his eyes on Dallas. And the gun barrels swung in to cover the gunfighter.

'S'pose you'd give me an argument if I said I'm gonna look into this – and I want you to hand over your gun.'

'I'd feel obliged to, Sheriff. It was a fair square-off. I can't help it if Harve was slower than he figured. I didn't want to draw on him.'

'You didn't try to talk him out of it!'

Dallas looked at the man who claimed Harve hadn't had a chance to drag his guns free of leather. 'Like I said, I've come up against a hundred like Harve. Soon as he backhanded the 'keep and busted his nose, I knew there was nowhere to go but slap leather. I'm damn tired, mister, and I didn't feel like arguing, so I got right to it.' He flicked his gaze to the sheriff. 'And that's the truth, Sheriff. If anyone thinks I shaded Harve, it was because I was way, *way* faster than he was, or could ever have hoped to be. That's not a boast: I'll show you if you want.'

'Don't touch that gun!' snapped Lake, the hammers cocking on the Greener. 'You – just hold it, Dallas!'

'I was gonna grab a shotglass from the bar and ask someone to drop it from waist level – I can shoot it long before it touches the floor.'

There were a few chuckles.

'Ain't no one *that* fast!'

'Well, we seen him down Harve, but Harve weren't near as slick as he figured – just faster'n anyone else in this town, but nowheres near as fast as Dallas.'

'Let him prove it, Arch,' a man called, and other voices joined in. 'Let Dallas *show* us he's fast as he says!'

Lake saw he was on a spot, agreed to it

only if Dallas handed his six-gun to the bartender who would remove all cartridges but one. And Lake would stand behind Dallas with the cocked shotgun.

Dallas shrugged, lifted his gun free of the holster by one finger and thumb on the stag-horn butt and dropped it onto the bartop. Burt unloaded it, pushed one cartridge back into the chamber.

'Make sure that chamber's on the bot-tom!' warned Lake, taking no chances.

Dallas smiled faintly as he took the gun, turned the cylinder by hand so that the loaded chamber would come up ready to fire when he cocked the hammer, dropped the Colt into his holster and turned his back on the sheriff. He looked at the man who had first claimed Harve hadn't been given a chance.

'Drop that glass whenever you're ready, friend. Don't have to be waist-level, just extend your arm down as far as it'll go and open your fingers.

The man was sweating, licked his lips as

he picked up the shotglass. 'Listen, I – I just wanted things to be fair!'

'Sure. I just done this town a favour by downing Harve, but let's make sure I done it fair and square, huh?' He held up his left hand as the man started to stutter something. 'As if it damn well matters – forget it, mister, I ain't gonna shoot *you*. Just drop that glass and let's get this over with.'

The man let it go quickly and jumped back, yelling and throwing his hands up in front of his face as the shot crashed and the glass shattered bare inches from where he had released it.

Ears ringing from the gunshot, the crowd were silent at first, then everyone began speaking at once. Dallas turned slowly to face the sheriff, spread his arms, the empty, smoking gun held out to one side– *There you are, just like I said...*

Big Archie Lake closed his mouth with a snap, settled the butt of the shotgun against his hip. 'Well, I sure as hell don't want a man as fast as you are in my town, Dallas, whether or not you give Harve an even break.' The gun barrels jerked suddenly and knocked the six-gun from Dallas's hand. 'Lift 'em – and high! I'm gonna let Judge Samuels decide this.'

Dallas was lifting his arms with an exasperated sigh, but stopped the movement abruptly, grey, bullet eyes narrowing as he looked at the sheriff. 'Judge *Vernon* Samuels?'

Lake sharpened his look. 'None other – you know him?'

Dallas merely nodded, barely moving his head at all, hands still only half-raised. Sheriff Lake stepped in and jabbed the shotgun into his belly, doubling Dallas over. The lawman shoved him roughly so that he fell to one knee, dazed.

Big Arch glared around at the silent crowd, as if saying, *See? I ain't afraid of any fast gun.*

'Get up, Dallas. I got a nice draughty cell for you!'

2

Uneven Break

The newly constructed Yuma Territorial Prison stood on a high bluff overlooking the confluence of the Gila and Colorado Rivers in deep south-west Arizona.

But although cooling breezes often blew through the prison, down the granite corridors of the five-foot thick walls, few zephyrs ever reached the prisoners in the main building, even though some of the cells had a strap-iron door at either end, between narrow, towering stone walls.

But then, Yuma was not designed as a pleasure palace and the inmates were vastly different from holidaymakers. The youngest 'inhabitant' was only fourteen years old, while the oldest was a child-murderer of eighty-eight. There were many anti-social types in-between, even some women, though kept in a separate section of the prison.

Frank Dallas looked up at the thick, forbidding walls as he shuffled along in line with other miscreants, already dressed in striped prison garb, wrists and ankles in irons.

For a little while there, back in town, he had foolishly believed he might escape any kind of a prison sentence. Instead, here he was, facing five *years'* incarceration.

Thanks to Judge Vernon Samuels, a man he had once known long years back on the trail, a man he had done a favour for – and who, apparently, had a short memory...

They had let him languish in the Yuma jailhouse for a full week after Big Archie Lake had arrested him in the saloon for gunning down Harve Lester.

The sheriff had said nothing when he had locked Dallas in his cell, except to warn him to: 'Behave – and you might get off with a couple of weeks' work on the county chain gang'.

That would have been acceptable to Dallas, figuring the judge would have to make some sort of a showing, but – five *years!*

He still could not believe the way it had happened...

The night deputy was a surly, tough, hard-case professional and apart from bringing Dallas some supper each night at six o'clock said nothing until he was relieved by the day man around five the next morning. The day deputy was a young *hombre,* no more than twenty, leery of Dallas – after no doubt hearing about his overblown reputation around town and yet, at the same time, he watched every move the gunfighter made. Not in an edgy, finger-on-the-trigger way, but with a certain almost reluctant admiration.

'You know Harve Lester?' Dallas asked one lunchtime, as the kid handed him his tin plate of beans floating in a thin sauce with a hunk of corn-pone and piece of nameless, half-cooked meat.

The deputy stepped back quickly and took a few moments to answer. He nodded, licking his lips. 'He weren't no friend – Harve never had *any* friends in this town. He was a troublemaker.'

'Won't be missed, huh?'

'Nope. That's for certain sure.' The kid was gathering confidence, fumbled to roll a cigarette, hesitated, then handed the tobacco sack and papers through the bars.

'Thanks, kid. What's your name?'

'Howie Roscoe. The sheriff's my uncle.'

Dallas nodded, licked the cigarette paper and rolled the smoke, sharing a match with Roscoe. 'Where's Big Arch now?'

The kid seemed uncomfortable. 'Takin' statements. From fellers that was in the saloon bar when you shot Harve.'

Dallas paused with the cigarette almost touching his lips. 'There's gonna be a court case then?'

'Aw, yeah – Judge Samuels'd insist on it. A real stickler for the letter-of-the-law is the judge.'

Howie Roscoe looked around quickly as if he was afraid someone might have overheard him, but the drunk in the cell next to Dallas was still deep down in an alcoholic dream that brought moans bordering on screams from his lips as he tossed and turned on the narrow bunk.

Dallas finished eating, glanced up.

'Judge Samuels – he's a by-the-book man now?' Dallas asked.

'Hell, yeah! There ain't a drunk gets off when the judge is holdin' court – and you spit on the street, you can count on a week or two on the chain gang.'

Dallas swore under his breath. 'Must've changed.'

'You know him?'

Dallas drew deeply on his cigarette, his eyes seeming far away. 'Thought I did, once.'

The judge had changed in looks when Dallas finally got to meet him in the Yuma Courthouse. He was fifteen years older, of course – must be fifty-plus – and had streaks of grey in his thick hair, deep lines on his jowly face, and his eyes were hard and unforgiving. The jaw was set like carved stone and he sat hunched over his bench, looking up from under heavy eyebrows as Dallas was led into the court.

The gavel banged and the skinny clerk of the court jumped up with his slicked-back hair and announced that the court of Judge Vernon Samuels was now in session, that all cigarettes should be extinguished immediately, any juice from chawing tobacco spat into the spittoons provided, and any noise would see the perpetrator being heavily fined and, if there was any protest at the fine, that person could count on time spent on the chain gang.

Dallas shook his head slowly: *Things sure had changed, all right.*

It was at about that time that his hope of a

lenient sentence flew out of the window with the burning cigarettes flicked out by the smokers in the crowd.

Twenty minutes later, he *knew* he was headed for the penitentiary: Lake had found three witnesses who claimed that Harve Lester hadn't even been given a chance to start his draw when Dallas had gunned him down.

'I deny that allegation,' spoke up Dallas, despite Lake's surly deputy growling at him to be quiet. 'But in any case, damned if I can see that it matters much. From what I gather, Harve Lester was a mean son of a bitch who–'

'Shut down that prisoner, Sheriff!' snapped Judge Samuels, eyes blazing, gavel pounding the bench. 'This instant!'

Big Arch rapped Dallas across the head with his Colt barrel – actually *Dallas's* Colt barrel – and the gunfighter swayed, grabbed at the dock railing to keep his feet, blinking. The gavel pointed at him.

'Another outburst like that, prisoner, and

you'll be gagged and forcibly restrained ... clear?'

Dallas, grey bullet eyes coming into cold focus now, nodded briefly. He held the judge's gaze until the man scowled and looked away.

The case continued, Dallas's past was read out – and not much of it was authentic. Mostly it was a mixture of legend and hearsay. He sounded like a mad-dog killer.

'I'd be seventy-three years old if I'd done all them things, judge!' he said, and the sheriff moved in but Samuels held up a hand.

'I believe I know Mr Dallas's record of gunfighting and killing, thank you, Sheriff. Perhaps more accurately than you do.'

The sheriff nodded, read out a little more and ended with, 'Judge, we all know Harve Lester was a pain in the – was no damn good, but I don't like no stranger sashayin' into our town and thinkin' he can gun down just anyone he pleases without even givin' 'em a chance.'

There were a few murmurings from the crowd but most folk seemed too afraid to make a sound in Samuels' presence.

The judge glared at Dallas. 'You have anything to say for yourself?'

'Only that these so-called witnesses are mistaken, Judge. I demonstrated my gun speed in the bar, and without breaking my arm trying to pat myself on the back, I'm here to tell you that I was just so much blamed faster on the draw than good ol' Harve that it just *seemed* like he hadn't made a start.'

'I think that would be exaggerating things considerably,' Samuels said with a sneer.

'Gimme a gun now, Judge, and I'll be glad to—'

'You'll be quiet! That is what you will be!' Samuels hunched his heavy shoulders as he glared at the prisoner.

Dallas narrowed his gaze. 'Like to approach the bench, Judge.'

Samuels reared back, blinked, startled at such a suggestion. The crowd seemed to hold its collective breath.

'You – what?' demanded the judge.

'Like to talk to you in confidence for a minute, Judge,' Dallas said quietly, gaze unwavering from the judge's flushed face. 'Or, if you want, I can just start in from here...'

Some folk thought the judge was going to throw a fit, his face darkened so much. He seemed to be trying to snap the carved handle on his gavel. Then some of the blood drained out of his face and he cleared his throat and gestured to Dallas to approach the bench.

The courtroom sighed in disbelief.

Dallas started to make his way out of the dock.

'Not you, Sheriff!' Samuels snapped, as the lawman made to accompany the prisoner. 'Just him.'

This was so much out of character for Samuels that there was a drumming murmur running through the crowd that only subsided after the gavel's hammerhead started to chew splinters out of the edge of the wooden block.

Dallas, manacled, shackled, shuffled up to stand in front of the high bench. Samuels had to half-rise out of his chair to hear what Dallas had to say.

'Just two words, Judge: Deadwood, South Dakota – OK, *three* words. Or I could add, *fifteen years ago* ... need to go on?'

'Yes! Yes, you son of a bitch, you *do* need to go on!' the judge hissed, and he shook a thick forefinger down at Dallas. 'And be very careful what you say, Mr Dallas – this is *my* courtroom and I will not be threatened!'

'Dunno that I need to say anything more, Judge. You ought to recollect what I'm talking about.'

'Of course, I do, you cheap shootist! I was only an attorney-at-law then! Part of a syndicate who had the good of the town at heart when we hired you to clean it up because no one would take on the sheriff's job ... am I *recollecting* to your satisfaction?'

Dallas, very sober now, his eyes holding the judge's gaze steadily, nodded gently. 'Far as it goes. But I also recollect that it was a mistake. Because most of the folk didn't *want* Deadwood cleaned up. They were making too much money the way it was – and it was a hell-hole with murder and rape and robbery running wild. I thought I was doing pretty good until you told me to stop, be satisfied with what I'd already been paid and to light on out.'

He was surprised to see Samuels' face flush again, but not, this time, with anger.

More like embarrassment. And a touch of – shame?

'Look, Dallas, that was a long time ago, a very long time ago. I was ambitious, didn't care what I had to do to get to the top, but – well, I saw the error of my ways, saw that if I was going to be a student of the law of the land, then *I* had to be exemplary in my behaviour.' Then the craggy jaw hardened and the eyes flashed. 'And I *have* been and I intend to go on setting a good example –

which is why my court goes by the book! And I make no exceptions.'

Dallas started to speak, but the heavy forefinger wagged in front of his eyes again.

'No! For your own good, Mr Dallas, do – not – say – what – you – are – thinking! Or, I promise you, you will find yourself behind the walls of the Territorial Prison for a minimum of ten years!'

That really shocked Dallas. 'How can that be going by the book, judge?' he asked bitterly. 'It was self-defence!'

Samuels sat back, a smug look on his face now and he lifted his voice to normal. 'You don't seem to realize, Mr Dallas, that a man has died because of your behaviour. No matter that he wasn't a good man, he was a human being, and we hold human life in high regard in our town. I must make an example of you so as to deter other borderline law-breakers from doing the same thing – you understand?'

'Look, Judge,' cut in Dallas, sounding a mite more desperate than he meant to.

'Judge, I'm tired, bone-weary, I've been trying to get settled someplace for years. Every time I think I've found the right place, some two-bit turkey-cock recognizes me and wants to make a name for himself by out-shooting me.'

'I've heard of such things,' Samuels said tightly, not too interested. 'I have no sympathy for you.'

'Not looking for any – what I'm saying is, I was on my way to California when I stopped here for a drink and to get some supplies to see me through the desert... I didn't come looking for trouble. Fact is, I haven't *looked* for trouble for years.'

'But it's always found you, eh?'

'That's about the size of it, Judge.'

'Well, it's a hard-luck story, I agree, but it's not in my power to change the way your luck runs. In my view, a man makes his own luck, good or bad. Now your main trouble, Dallas, is that you acted too willingly, were too *ready* to kill your man, so I'm going to sentence you to five years in Yuma Penitentiary.'

There was dead silence in court.

Judge Samuels looked at the gunfighter with a certain amount of triumph. Frank Dallas stared back blankly.

He couldn't think of a damn thing to say as the big sheriff led him away roughly by the arm, pushing, shoving.

What the hell had he expected anyway? Hell, once he would've seen mighty early in the piece that he was getting the good old heave-ho just to make the goddamn judge look good. He was tired, all right. Or getting to be an old man at forty-two...

But he'd be a lot older when he came out of Yuma: prison years had a way of ageing a man way beyond the same time spent outside the high stone walls...

Judge Vernon Samuels adjusted his black robe, easing his neck within the collar, rapped his gavel twice and called irritably, 'Next case!'

Now here was Frank Dallas, one-time gunfighter, entering the main gate beneath the large watchtower full of guards with their special four-muzzled Lowell battery guns covering the prisoners, shuffling into a new world between high, thick granite-block walls, the *only* world he would know for the next five years.

Thanks to Judge Vernon Samuels getting religion...

Funny, but the thing Dallas remembered best of the sham of a trial was the judge speaking just as the deputy led him down into the underground cell block beneath the court:

'Clerk, hurry things along a little, will you? My daughter is arriving on the afternoon steamboat from Phoenix with my brand-new grandson, young Vernon Samuel Beldon, and I'm anxious to see the little fellow, being my first grandchild...'

Just for a few minutes there, the judge had sounded almost human, thought Dallas, as he was shoved into his cell, a long narrow room ten feet by six, carved out of the living rock of the bluff and sealing him off from the world outside by a heavy, strap-iron door.

Well, reformed characters always were the worst kind, he allowed.

The crash of the bolt shooting across and being locked into its socket by the silent guard sounded like an executioner's gunshot.

3

Firebrand

The trio of riders hit Yuma after dark. It was bitterly cold, this being early winter now.

Todd Yancey was in a foul mood: he hated cold, and he could have been home on the ranch back in the Tonto Basin, warming his feet in front of the big fireplace, watching the shapes and demons leaping in the flames, instead of freezing his butt off in this dump.

Blame the Old Man. Yeah!

His father, Solomon Yancey, was the one responsible. Happened to be in an ornery mood when the trail boss of the big herd that had followed them into Tucson came to complain.

'Judas, Yancey, we all know you got a

reputation for being an ornery sonuver, and you figure your money'll buy any damn thing you want, but I'm here to tell you it ain't gonna buy that kid of yours no favours this time!'

The trail boss was from a spread up on the Muggyown – officially called the Mogollon Rim – and he headed-up a kind of cattlemen's alliance, several ranchers having pooled their round-up steers for the drive into Tucson. The man had some hard backing, but he didn't scare Solomon Yancey who was used to getting his own way.

'Look, Cooney, or whatever your name is, it was an accident, that fire–'

Cooney scoffed and spat. *Accident!* Like hell it was! That kid of yours come sniffin' around the daughter of one of our ranchers – she's only fourteen, for Chris'sakes! He got his ass kicked and was lucky at that. When he found out our herd was trailin' yours and some of the cows belonged to the gal's father, the little shit set fire to the graze after your herd'd passed through it.'

Solomon Yancey wasn't a big man physically, but he was one of the toughest cattlemen in Arizona – if not the rest of the United States. He was blocky of build, with a chest thick through as a tallow cask, hands that could knot-up into fists as hard as an anvil. His eyes were an ice blue, a little rheumy now he was in his sixties, but with a deadly cast that many a man had quavered before.

Cooney didn't flinch as they settled on his craggy face. Yancey remained silent a moment longer.

'Cooney, I simply ain't gonna stand here and listen to you bad-mouth my son. You get on back to your herd and if you got any sense you'll find another route to Tucson, one that has plenty of graze. My boy dropped a bottle of coal oil and it ran downhill into the remains of a brandin' fire which started the main blaze. Got away from us, that's all.'

Cooney looked more sceptical than ever

but shifted his gaze when he caught a small movement to his left. He sucked in a sharp breath. He knew that dark shape silhouetted against the chuck wagon's canvas – a lot of men had recognized it, but quite a few wouldn't be able to tell you about it. Unless you could contact the dead...

Bo Kirby, Solomon Yancey's bodyguard. And damned if that feller standing beside him wasn't the kid himself, Todd Yancey!

They didn't have to say anything. Cooney knew the only thing he could do was retreat with his tail tucked up between his legs. No one in their right mind would deliberately tangle with Bo Kirby.

He scowled at Solomon. 'All right! I ain't stupid enough to call out Kirby, but you ain't heard the last of this, Yancey! Not by a damn sight! That kid of yours has gotten away with murder in the past, but he ain't gettin' off with this! We lost over forty cows, seven hosses and I got eleven men laid-up with burns or stove-in ribs!'

'See him on his way, Bo,' Solomon Yancey

said casually and turned away, tucking his napkin into his shirt collar again as he sat down on a tree stump and picked up his tin plate of food, swearing because his supper was now cold.

Bo Kirby moved to intercept Cooney as the man started to sprint for his horse, cursing the rage and stupidity that had allowed him to ride into the Yancey trail camp alone.

He didn't make the horse.

Kirby caught up with him and spun him around. Cooney was no slouch in a fight and started swinging immediately. He even landed a couple of blows that jolted the gunman, then Kirby head-butted him in the face and, as Cooney stumbled back, he kicked the man's legs out from under him.

That finished Cooney. Before Kirby had got in more than a couple of licks with his boots, Todd Yancey was there right alongside him, kicking brutally, grunting with his effort, turning so he could rake with his spurs...

By the time they lashed the bleeding, battered Cooney to his horse, he was unconscious and sagging in the saddle. Bo Kirby snapped his fingers at one of the silent trail hands who left his supper and started to lead the horse and its grisly burden away from the camp.

Solomon Yancey wiped his greasy mouth on the napkin, standing slowly, his head appearing too large for his squat body now as he ran his hands through twine-coloured hair.

'Boy,' he snapped at his son, who was helping himself to another slice of deep-dish apple pie. Todd looked around kind of irritably. 'There's gonna be trouble over this. I can handle it or have it handled, but not if you're around to remind them Muggyowns just how you thumbed your nose at 'em.'

'What you saying, Pop?' Todd was in his early twenties, wolf-faced, rangy, not bad-looking, and he could smile the snarl off a grizzly when he set his mind to it. But now he tried to look suitably contrite, having no wish to rile the Old Man any more than he already had.

'I'm sayin' I'm sendin' you, with Vinnie and Buck to look out for you, to Yuma... Hush up till I'm finished damn you, boy! Your damn shenanigans are gonna cost me a lot of money to square away. Now you listen and don't argue... I've had me a gutful of talkin'. You just do like I say – you, Vinnie and Buck are goin' to Yuma. Cattle are comin' down the river on the steamboats. You buy a few hundred and you drive 'em back to the Tonto Basin – the long way round.' Solomon bored his ice-cold eyes into the kid who seemed hard-pressed not to protest. 'You stay way south of Casa Grande, till you get to San Manuel, then follow the San Pedro back to the Basin.'

'Hell's teeth!' exploded Todd, unable to restrain himself any longer. 'We'll be into mid-winter by then! And we don't need any more cows, Pop! Specially that Californian stuff we'd pick up in Yuma.'

'Glad to see you're interested enough to figure that out. Nonetheless, that's what you're gonna do, and by the time you get back, I ought to have them Muggyowns settled down an' not lookin' to nail your hide to the barn door.'

Well, that was that. There was no arguing with Sol Yancey when he was in that kind of mood.

So here they were now, arriving after dark with a bitter devil-wind cutting through their clothing and squeezing the tears from the corners of their eyes.

'Let's find us a roomin'-house and get bedded down for the night,' said Buck Davis, teeth chattering. 'Reckon I'll cuddle up to a bottle of redeye to keep me warm.'

'Not me,' said Todd, and his words brought Vinnie Cranston's head up sharply.

'Now, come on, Todd!' he said quickly. 'You ain't got no notion of hittin' the high-spots tonight have you?'

'High-spots? In this dump? You've got to

be kidding, Vin. But there's gotta be at least *one* whorehouse and I figure we got enough money to buy something a lot better than a bottle of rotgut whiskey to keep us warm.'

'Whoa, man! That's Sol's money – for buyin' cows,' warned Vinnie Cranston, starting to feel sicker by the minute. He just damn well *knew* this was how the lousy chore was going to work out! He'd been sent to ride herd on this loco kid before and it had always ended in trouble, sometimes just a fine – paid for by Solomon, of course – but there had been shootings and, once, a slashing, and a couple of beatings that had left a man and a woman near-crippled.

Why hadn't he had the guts to tell Solomon he didn't want the damn job of wet-nursing his crazy son?

Too late now, though.

Todd Yancey grinned tightly with his even white teeth, sensing the uneasiness of the others and getting a kick out of it. 'Boys, I feel a leetle wild tonight. Let's find us a whorehouse and see what they got to offer.

If it ain't what we want, why, we'll just change a few things until it is. You with me?'

'I dunno about this, Todd,' grumbled Buck, but Vinnie Cranston merely heaved a sigh.

'For Chris'sakes don't kill any of the damn whores! I got no notion to see the inside of that Yuma Pen.'

'Hell, we're just gonna have a little fun is all,' Todd assured him, feeling better already. 'Even a dump like this can't begrudge a trail hand a little cutting loose.'

Three hours later, Todd Yancey learned that Yuma could indeed begrudge *his* kind of trail hand *his* kind of fun.

By then, the whorehouse on Simms Street was in flames and a woman was screaming endlessly.

Vinnie Cranston was still buckling his trousers when he ran along the hallway to the room where the screams were coming from.

Todd Yancey stood inside, hitching up his own trousers, while a bleach-haired whore rolled about the bed, clawing at her naked breasts which were blotched with burns, no doubt caused by the cigar held between Todd's teeth.

Yancey glared at Cranston. 'The bitch wouldn't do what I wanted and threatened to call the bouncer, so I taught her a lesson ... let's get outa here!'

'Christ, kid, we'd better!' Vinnie snapped, drawing his gun as the door burst open and two hard-faced men in tight vests and trousers burst in, swinging wooden clubs.

Cranston dropped the first man with a vicious swing of his gun but the weapon jarred from his hand and, as he stooped to pick it up, the second man closed.

Todd Yancey shot him, the man howling as he twisted away and fell in a heap in the passage.

'That's done it!' yelled Vinnie, scooping up his Colt, grabbing Yancey by the arm and pushing him towards the window.

Yancey curled a lip, adrenalin surging, wanting more action. As he staggered past the bed he struck out at the screaming girl, the foresight of his gun raking across her face and neck. Her screams intensified, and Vinnie Cranston shot at men who started to cram into the room. They scattered, and Todd, eyes alight now, swept the burning oil lamp off the bedside table and onto the bed. A bullet from his gun smashed it and hot oil sprayed over the writhing girl's legs. Moments later the bed was blazing.

Todd Yancey whooped and hollered and Vinnie practically threw him out of the window, emptying his gun towards the door as he flung a leg over the sill.

There was a balcony and they ran along it towards stairs that led down one side of the timber building. Whores and their customers were poking heads out of windows as the two men rushed by, then hurriedly withdrew into their rooms.

Yancey stopped dead, dodged around the reaching Cranston, and went to the nearest window. He shot out the oil lamp inside and another room was on fire in seconds. Vinnie shoved him so hard he half-fell down the stairs, clattering. But Yancey was on his high now, laughing, eyes bright, enjoying himself. He howled like a wolf.

Cranston got him away from the whorehouse before he did any more damage. It was going to be too late to save it anyway and there was already a big crowd of onlookers in the street. Someone was yelling for the local volunteer fire crew and Yancey, panting in the shadows, with Vinnie holding him back against the wall, suddenly lurched, brought up his knee into Cranston's groin, and ran back to join the crowd staring at the blazing whorehouse where someone still screamed. Yancey's face was ecstatic...

Big Archie Lake grabbed him ten minutes later when the dishevelled whorehouse madam recognized Yancey. He had a wide grin on his face, was half-dancing in pleasure as he watched the building burn and the frantic efforts of most of the townsfolk to stop the blaze from spreading.

'You lousy bastard!' Lake snapped, and bent his gun-barrel over Todd Yancey's head.

He caught the man as he crumpled and flung him over one beefy shoulder. 'I'll keep him in the cells till Judge Samuels is ready for him tomorrow,' the sheriff said and the madam slapped the unconscious Todd's face, tears streaming down her face as she cursed him bitterly.

Vinnie, still clutching his aching genitals, watched silently from the shadows as the lawman carried Todd down towards the jailhouse.

Buck Davis came up out of a whiskey-induced sleep to hear the pounding on the door of his room. His head was thick and woozy and his belly felt rough and queasy from the rotgut he had consumed.

'All right, all *right!*' he snarled, rolling out of bed and padding barefoot across the cold linoleum floor, rubbing his hands: he'd forgotten it was a cold night.

50

He unlocked the door and stumbled back as Vinnie Cranston staggered in, looking wild-eyed and smelling of woodsmoke.

'The hell–'

Vinnie grabbed Buck's underwear up close to his throat and shook the man, slamming him back against the wall.

'Judas, Vinnie! What've I done?'

'Shut your whinin' and listen!' panted Vinnie, kicking the door closed. 'The kid's busted loose again! *Shut up!* Burned a whore then burned down the goddamn cat-house! You musta slept through it. Looks like a few people died in the fire. Now, listen, this's what you do. You send a telegraph to Sol, sayin' what's happened ... no, wait! From what I can find out, the kid's up before judge Samuels tomorrow. See what happens in court, *then* wire Sol. Savvy?'

Buck Davis was struggling although he was fully awake now. His belly was churning worse than ever, his heart pounding. 'Hell, the Old Man'll have our nuts for lettin' this happen!'

Vinnie was nodding impatiently. 'You know what to do?' He shook Buck again and the man knocked his hand away irritably.

'Said I did – now cut it out! But you oughta be the one to send the wire, he put you in charge of the kid.'

Vinnie grinned tightly. '*You* send it. I won't be around.'

Buck blinked. 'Huh? What the hell you mean...?'

'*Do it, Buck!* I ain't stickin' around to see what Sol aims to do. *Adios!*'

Vinnie Cranston swung to the door, opened it and went out without looking back. Buck stood there shivering, realizing he had been left holding the hot end of the branding-iron and not liking it one damn bit.

Judge Vernon Samuels set those deadly eyes on Todd Yancey as the young man stood in the dock, manacled hands and feet. The kid didn't look in any way remorseful, only cocky.

'You sorry for what you done, son?' Samuels asked quietly, all eyes in the courtroom on him now.

'I don't remember anything, Judge,' Yancey said, in such a way that even the dumbest man in that room could tell it was something he had said a hundred times before.

'You suffer with mental blackouts, boy?'

'Yessir – I'm not responsible for my actions during such time – and, Judge, if you'd just hold off until my father can send down his attorney – Roderick Ball of Ball, Ball and Dickey.'

'I know Mr Ball and his reputation for getting rich folk out of trouble so they don't have to be responsible for their actions,' cut in Samuels coldly. 'But it's no good you waiting for an attorney, son, because I'm not *going* to wait. Too many witnesses saw what you did, saw you *enjoying* yourself. You don't have *any* defence!'

'Hell, I was drunk–'

'*Quiet,* damn you!' The judge leaned

halfway across his bench, face colouring, gavel smashing on to the block.

The kid reared back in the dock and his face went white. For the first time, he realized that he was in real trouble with this by-the-book judge. His father was too far away to help him. Vinnie was missing and Buck hadn't been near him.

For the first time, he was alone, and it scared him white...

The judge was still talking, haranguing him for his behaviour as being not only irresponsible but downright murderous.

'You sound like you've had education, boy, but being a rich man's son, I guess that's to be expected. It should've given you a much better sense of responsibility. And I know your father's reputation, too, but it won't help you. Two young women died in that fire, as well as a male citizen of this town, and other good people were injured because of your actions, boy! Now you got to pay for what you did!'

'Judge, I'm sorry. I can't help these

blackouts. My doctor would explain if I could send for him...'

'I'm sure he would, Mr Yancey. As no doubt your attorney would do his best to *explain* your reprehensible behaviour – if he were here.'

'But, Judge!' Yancey sounded quite desperate now. 'I'm not *responsible* when I suffer these blackouts!'

'Well, this time I'm *making* you responsible!' Samuels wagged a thick forefinger. 'You *will* pay for what you have done – and pay dearly, I promise you!'

Solomon Yancey was studying the well-worn playing cards in his heavy hands, a thick cigar jutting from a corner of his mouth, the smoke mingling with clouds of more tobacco smoke hanging fog-like above the table.

The other five players waited, some impatiently, others knowing Sol Yancey of old, how he liked to drag out the deal, keep them all sweating until he made up his mind what to do: call, fold, or merely smile crookedly, and spread out the cards saying – always the same words – *'Read 'em and weep, gents, read 'em and weep!'*

But this night, he didn't do any of those things.

A man came into the private room at the back of the Silverwing Saloon on Tucson's notorious Cornshuck Street, closed the door gently behind him and stood at the edge of the table holding a folded paper in his hands.

Yancey frowned as he glanced up, then turned back to studying his cards. One of the other poker players gestured to the newcomer, a gangling man wearing suspenders on his shirtsleeves and cardboard cuff protectors. The man stepped across, leaned down and whispered in the player's ear.

The gambler smiled as he looked up. 'Sorry to break your concentration, Sol, but this gentleman has a message for you. Says it's important.'

Yancey scowled around his cigar, glaring at the nervous newcomer. 'At ten o'clock at night? What the hell can be that important he has to come in here and interrupt our game?'

A couple of the others nodded and murmured their own protests, but the man, nervous still, but unfazed, moved around the table and held out his piece of folded paper. Immediately, Yancey recognized the unmistakable yellow of a telegraph message form. He flicked his gaze to the messenger's sweating face.

'Sounded right urgent, Mr Yancey. Thought I'd best bring it round right away.'

Yancey snatched the form without taking his eyes off the man, unfolding the paper, finally lowering his gaze to read the printed words.

TODD SENTENCED TO TEN YEARS YUMA PEN BY JUDGE VERNON SAMUELS. VINNIE RUN OUT. I QUIT. SORRY. BUCK DAVIS.

Yancey stood slowly, staring at the words, lips moving slightly as he reread them. The others were silent now, watching the barrel-chested rancher, his face bloodless.

'Anything we can help with, Sol?' one man asked, stroking his moustache.

Yancey snapped up his head, crumpling the message form and stuffing it into his pocket. He lifted his jacket off the back of his chair and the messenger stepped forward swiftly and held it for him. As the rancher slipped his arms through the sleeves, the messenger said, 'I hope I did the right thing, Mr Yancey.'

Sol Yancey grunted, felt in his waistcoat pocket, then reached for the pile of money on the table before his chair and picked up a gold double eagle, flicking it towards the man who caught it deftly, his mouth agape.

'You did – and that's to make sure you *continue* to do the right thing. Savvy?'

The messenger understood right away: the double eagle plainly said, *Keep your mouth shut about the telegraph's contents.*

Yancey jerked his head and the man hurried for the door. The other players looked disappointed as Yancey scooped up his money and bared his teeth around his cigar.

'Deal me out, gents. My apologies. 'Night.'

'Wait up, Sol! Maybe we can help.'

'Thanks all the same, but no thanks.' Yancey went out into the night and flung away his cigar hurriedly, striding down towards his hotel where Bo Kirby would be dozing in a chair, awaiting his return or summons.

The gunfighter came wide awake on the instant when the rancher entered, and Kirby saw immediately by the man's face that there was trouble. He read the crumpled telegraph message swiftly, swore as he looked up.

He was just an average-sized man, in his thirties, well built, had a rugged kind of face that most people recognized right off as pitiless, once they'd looked into his dark eyes. His clothes were good quality as was the supple black leather of his gun rig.

'That goddamn Vinnie!' he hissed.

'Yeah. Runnin' off like that. Get Zack and Mohawk on his trail! Don't care how long it takes, but they're to bring him back. Don't matter if he's beat-up or shot-up, long as he's alive enough so's he'll know it's me who's finishin' him off. Forget Buck: Vinnie was the one s'posed to be in charge.'

Bo Kirby frowned. 'Vinnie's got to be taken care of, Sol, sure, but the boy ought to be first on the list.'

'*I know that!*' roared Yancey. 'When you've sent Zack and Mohawk after Vinnie, you get a wire away to Roderick Ball and tell him to meet me in Yuma, pronto. Then get you and me on the first train out.'

Kirby looked uncertain. 'The train only runs once a week to Yuma, Sol, and it went yesterday.'

Jesus Christ! *I don't care!* Hire a loco and a private car if you have to, find us a place in a box car with a load of cows. Do whatever you need to – just get me to Tucson. I'll show this son of a bitch of a judge just what he's up against, sending *my* son to the Pen for ten goddamn years!'

'On my way, Sol.' Kirby grabbed hat and jacket, making for the door.

Yancey slumped into a chair and rubbed his eyes.

4

Yuma

Dallas had been six months in Yuma and the bitter winds of early winter were turning the place into an ice box. The prisoners were issued with extra blankets and warmer clothing, all of which were inadequate.

But at least Warden Luckett attempted to give his charges some comfort. As it turned out, Luckett was a strange mixture of hair-trigger temper and humanity. He had fought to have a dentist call at the prison fairly regularly to examine and treat the dental problems of the inmates. He ordered gardens dug and maintained and vegetable crops planted, some of the produce already stored in underground cellars for the coming winter. He even had a library stocked, picked some scholarly types from amongst his charges, and for those men who wanted it, there were reading and writing classes, and even an elementary school curriculum.

The classes weren't popular at first, but then even some of the toughest hardcases began to wander in and learn their ABC and a little of the Three Rs. The food was tolerable – better than some of these men had known during their earlier lives – and the doctor was a concerned individual, not the usual rummy living out his days in the prison system as was often the case.

Luckett would even listen to men's grievances and, if they were genuine and it was within his power, he would correct them, at least in a token way. But if they were frivolous and he figured the complainant was wasting his time, that misguided prisoner would find himself doing serious time in the Dark Cell which was little more than a cramped iron cage set in the granite, no light, no sound, for it was deep within the rock, no conversation, one meal a day and water, and nothing but a thin straw pallet to sleep on.

Yes, Luckett had a strict side to him, too – some called it *mean*, others *ornery*, but the fact was, Yuma was not the hellhole that rumour would have it. Not that the inmates didn't have to work – and work hard – for their privileges, but as long as they met the reasonable quotas set by Warden Luckett, they could depend on halfway decent food and fair treatment. There were beatings, of course, by the guards, and the bad ones were the subject of an inquiry headed up by Luckett himself. Sometimes the guards found themselves doing a little time in the Dark Cell.

'Discipline I will have,' Luckett was fond of saying, 'brutality I will not. Any man who can't control these men with a minimum of violence will soon find himself one of their number.'

In most cases this was enough to deter excess brutality, but it still went on occasionally and the victims with visible signs were intimidated so that they claimed they had been hurt in work-related accidents.

Luckett may or may not have been fooled by this, but often the guard responsible would find himself transferred out without explanation. If a man was foolish enough to attempt escape – a virtual impossibility – and he was recaptured as was the normal thing, he could bet on a long time in the Dark Cell and when he came out, he would shuffle and struggle back to his workplace carrying a thirty-pound ball and chain that would stay on until Luckett said 'enough'. Trouble amongst the prisoners themselves was a different matter altogether.

The guards would look the other way, quite happy to allow the prisoners to beat-up on each other. If it got bad enough for someone to need hospital treatment, then they would report the fight, but usually Luckett's interrogation was so thorough that it was simply easier to say that it had happened on the guard's coffee break and he had seen nothing.

Luckett also tended to turn a blind eye, unless there was real mayhem and murder involved. He believed in allowing prisoners to settle their differences in their own way. Only up to a point, though. Beyond that point lay Hell itself.

And, as in any prison, there was a pecking order, and whoever was at the top had to be prepared to fight to stay there because there were some mighty ornery outlaws within the granite walls of Yuma Territorial Prison in the late 1870s.

There was a killer named 'Dutch' Holland. An outlaw for many years and wanted in several States of the Union, he had been caught in Arizona where, fortunately for him, there were no murder charges against him, although he was supposed to have killed more than a dozen people in various other places during his career.

But Judge Samuels, going by the book as usual, said he must first pay for his crimes committed in Arizona and if he was still alive at the end of his twenty-year sentence, then he would be extradited to one of the States that wanted him for murder.

It didn't take Dutch long to establish himself as king-pin in Yuma, surrounded by half-a-dozen lackeys who would do his bidding. But the prisoners in the main were comfortable enough and rarely did Dutch have to do anything more than make his demands and they would be complied with. No one wanted to go up against him, but more than that, no one wanted to lose Luckett's privileges, either, so they simply avoided trouble by doing mostly what Dutch said.

This caused a little frustration to Dutch because he was a mean and vicious man and he liked trouble, *wanted* others to defy him so he would have an excuse to show his power. But he was quick to cover, too, and it was usually one of his hangers-on who took any punishment meted out by Luckett.

But while Dutch enjoyed an almost luxurious existence in Yuma, there was one thorn in his side that gave him a whole slew of aggravation.

The 'thorn's' name was Frank Dallas.

Not only was Dutch unable to bend the man to his will, Dallas showed him absolutely no respect and refused to be provoked by his hardcases. Except the time Fizz McMasters made the mistake of deliberately tripping Dallas in the yard and not only laughing about it but kicking muddy water from a puddle into Dallas's face.

The gunfighter had gotten slowly to his feet and Fizz had said, loudly, 'Hey, old man, the cold gettin' into your bones?'

Dallas looked at the torn skin on his mud-caked hands where they had skidded across the gravel, and then set those bullet eyes on McMasters. The man's laugh faded and he licked his lips as he took an involuntary step backwards. Then Dallas grinned.

'Could be, Fizz. Looks like the cold's making me clumsy anyway.'

He set off on his business, leaving

McMasters and two more of Holland's men frowning in puzzlement after him.

'He ain't yaller, I damn well know that,' one man allowed.

'Well, why din' he take a swing at me?'

'Mebbe he figured it wasn't worth it.'

'Hogwash. He *is* yaller!' McMasters couldn't leave well enough alone, hurried after Dallas, other prisoners getting out of his way quickly.

He reached for Dallas's shoulder, swung him round, opened his mouth to speak – and suddenly it was full of freezing mud and he was gagging and choking, staggering around in a weaving circle. Dallas wiped his hands on his prison clothes – already muddied from his fall – and continued on across the yard... Fizz continued to choke.

Dallas heard the guards running behind him but didn't look round. Later, he learned – the whole prison learned – that McMasters had choked to death, having inhaled a small quantity of the half-frozen mud: it took him several days to die of pleurisy complicated by pneumonia brought about by this incident. An unpleasant death for an unpleasant man.

Questioned by Luckett himself, prisoners in the yard swore McMasters had slipped and landed on his face in a puddle. Falls were always a hazard in this weather – just ask Frank Dallas, they told the warden. He may not have believed them, but he let it go for now.

Dutch Holland was quite a bit shaken by Fizz's sudden death.

He was a large man, a lazy man, and he didn't exert himself much these days. But Fizz had been kin of his and he felt duty bound to square things personally with Dallas over this.

'Skip,' he said to one of his men in the cell block the same night news of McMasters' death had come through, 'Dallas is mine. Spread the word. Leave him be. I gotta do some thinkin' on this first ... but won't be long before Frank Dallas is buried right alongside old Fizz on Cemetery Hill.'

As for Frank Dallas, he carried on with his normal routine prison life, apparently unaware or unworried about any revenge Dutch Holland might take.

It was certain sure that Fizz McMasters' death didn't cause him to lose any sleep.

The day that Dutch decided to take his revenge was the day that Todd Yancey arrived in Yuma Prison with a new intake of prisoners from all over the Territory.

Yancey was among half a dozen picked out of the line and told to grab an axe and/or a saw from the tool pile nearby and go where the armed guard told them to.

Todd Yancey didn't like the sound of it: hell, he hadn't even seen his cell yet! This was Judge goddam Samuels doing, he knew; give the warden a list of the real hardcases amongst the new intake and then set them to work right away on something that would exhaust them so they would be glad to tumble into their bunks at night, too blamed tired to make any trouble.

He had seen it work before on the other two occasions when he had been in jail. Solomon had gotten him out pronto and he had served no more than two weeks – this time should be no different, although – although there was a nagging hunch somewhere in the back of his head that Samuels was not a man to mess with. Hell, why worry? The Devil himself couldn't faze old Sol, so why should some backwater judge?

But there was still that uneasiness when he and the others were herded into the wood-yard and told to start sawing and splitting timber to be added to huge wall-like stacks already filling much of the yard. Several other prisoners were already at work and sawdust and woodchips were flying.

'You, Dallas,' the rough-voiced guard said to a tall man stripped to the waist, his hair cropped like everyone else in Yuma. 'Keep an eye on these greenhorns while I go have a smoke.'

Dallas nodded without looking up and the

newcomers shuffled away to start their clumsy assault on the huge stack of timber. Yancey managed to get close to Dallas.

'They were talking about you on the way up here – Frank Dallas, the gunfighter.'

Dallas flicked him a glance, continued splitting wood, sweat sheening his torso in the clear winter sunshine. Muscles rippled as the axe blade sliced through the hard wood.

'You *are* Dallas, aren't you?' Yancey asked a mite tightly when the man didn't answer.

'So?'

'Like to talk to you sometime, hear about all the gunfights you're s'posed to have walked away from.'

Dallas paused, leaning on his axe handle, breathing a little faster than usual. 'Forget the talk – start chopping wood.'

Todd Yancey's eyes narrowed and his knuckles whitened about the handle of his axe. 'You don't give me orders!'

'Someone better or you'll find out what the Dark Cell looks like.'

Todd curled a lip. 'That where the bogey-man lives?'

'Suit yourself,' Dallas said, shouldered the younger man aside, grabbed another section of wood and started splitting it.

'Listen, don't you lay your hands on me!' Todd growled, recovering his balance and making his way towards Dallas.

Without looking up, Dallas said quietly, 'You keep on coming, kid, and you'll lose a foot.'

Yancey stopped dead in his tracks, going white. Then a guard came running up, grabbed him by the shoulder and sent him staggering towards the huge pile of dead trees that had been dragged into the yard for cutting up.

'Get to work, greenhorn! *Now!*'

Yancey had enough good sense not to swing on the guard as his instincts told him to and, moving slowly as a mark of defiance, he set up a section of tree and began swinging his axe desultorily.

At the first chance, he slipped in amongst

the tangled tree trunks and found a small clear section and settled down, axe beside him. It was cold out of the sun and what little sweat he had raised began to chill on him but he didn't care. He smiled crookedly. *Hell, he could lick these yokels standing on his head drinking a cup of hot coffee.* They keep giving him opportunities like this and he might even start to enjoy his stay, have something to laugh over with the Old Man when he sprang him.

He settled down with a sigh, hidden by the fallen trees.

Dallas felt the change that had come over the woodyard. It came suddenly, like a draught when someone opened a door into a warm room. He wrenched his axe free of the log he was splitting and looked around.

The rough-voiced guard who had sneaked a smoke earlier, named Scottie, was standing on an earthen bank, looking kind of uneasily about him. Then, as Dallas watched, the man nodded to the guard who had dragged Yancey away and the man cleared his throat and called, 'All right – time for a break. Line up and march out to the adobe yard. We can shelter from the wind in the angle of the walls there.'

The prisoners stared at each other, at least the old hands did – the greenhorns simply threw down their tools with relief and started out of the yard. But the old hands couldn't believe it – there were no rest breaks in Yuma during the working day. *And* there was nothing like a cold wind blowing in here worthy of the name.

Dallas heard the sound of gravel crunching under heavy boots behind him. Scottie was standing there, rifle gripped tightly, beads of sweat on his face. The man ran a tongue around his lips.

'Not you, Dallas, you don't get a rest break. Just stay put.'

'What goes on?' Dallas asked.

The rifle swung over to cover him. 'Drop the axe, move over near the tree pile and – just wait. You move and I'll shoot you down and say you were making a run for it.'

Dallas's bleak stare visibly upset the guard and the man changed his grip on the rifle. He was nervous enough to shoot as threatened.

Frank Dallas dropped the axe into a half-split log and moved across to where Scottie directed. The others were being herded out of the yard and Scottie backed up and closed the gate – and then Dallas knew what was going on.

Big Dutch Holland had been standing hidden behind the open gate and he came lumbering forward now, the pale winter sunlight glinting from the blade he held low.

Dallas was far from any axe that he could grab and use as a weapon. The guard had put him in a narrow corner between two ten-foot high stacks of wood, trapping him neatly so there was no escape – except past Holland himself.

Dutch stopped a few feet away, grinning tightly, a clean-shaven man with thick, rubbery lips and beefy shoulders now hunched with the anticipation of driving that knife, made by Skip in the machine shop from a broken file, deep into Dallas's guts.

'I ever tell you Fizz was kin of mine? First cousin. You oughtn't've killed him, Dallas.'

'Seeing as he was likely acting on your orders, I figure you ought to take the blame, Dutch,' Dallas said easily, but his eyes weren't easy. They were narrowed and alert, watching the big man as one huge threat, ready for any sign that would warn he was about to attack.

'You piece of Texas dung! I been lookin' forward to this!'

Dutch was poised, ready to make his run when Dallas shook his head slowly, smiling faintly, confusing the man so that he stopped, started to lift his knife-hand again, then paused once more.

'Got it wrong, Dutch. I'm not from Texas... Dallas is a family name. Irish or English or something. I come from Dakota, place called Fargo in the north–'

Dutch swore savagely. 'Don't care where you *come* from! Only where you're *goin'*, and that's straight to *Hell!*'

As he started forward again Dallas leapt up onto the lowest tree trunk, ran along it and was above Dutch in a couple of seconds. Dutch turned, trying to make the movement in mid-stride, stumbled.

Then Dallas dived onto those heavy shoulders, driving with his muddy work boots. Dutch howled as he went down on his knees and his face smashed into the rough bark of one of the cut trees.

Dallas straddled him from behind, locked one arm about the man's neck, wrestled to grab the knife-hand. Dutch swung backwards and Dallas grunted as the blade sliced across his lower ribs, opening a gash, blood flowing. But he grabbed the hand and he twisted savagely, baring his teeth, stomping on Holland's spine as he wrenched upwards.

Bone cracked and Holland briefly passed out. By the time he came to his senses,

Dallas held the knife. Dutch sobbed as he lumbered to his feet, right hand dangling loosely, his face drawn with pain. He hurled himself at Dallas, despite the threatening blade, rammed his head into the gunfighter's chest. Being slippery with sweat still, Dutch's head slid upwards and cracked under Dallas's chin.

He staggered, knees buckling. Holland rammed a heavy shoulder into him, forcing him back against a tree, just missing a ragged, broken branch stub near his kidneys. He leaned into the dazed Dallas and snapped at the man's throat with his teeth. He missed but locked them into his shoulder.

Dallas writhed, trying to keep a grip on the slippery knife. He had known all along it was to be a fight to the death and he thought, irrelevantly, that it must have cost Dutch plenty to set it up...

Then he brought up his knee, once, twice, three times, each driving blow lifting Dutch to his toes. The man fell to his knees, gagging sickly. Dallas didn't hesitate, knowing the only way for this to end was for one of them to die.

And he didn't aim for it to be him.

He stood back, panting, swaying, one hand pressed against his side as he stared down at the bloody corpse sprawled at his feet, the knife buried to the hilt in Dutch Holland's chest. The man's eyes were open but lifeless, staring blankly up at the gunfighter.

He wiped sweat from his face.

He couldn't leave the body here, but he couldn't hide it among the dead trees for it would be discovered very quickly.

Too bad they weren't in the quarry, or at the blue claybank, digging out tons of the gooey clay ... he could bury Dutch there. But he *wasn't* there, and he had to get rid of Dutch fast. He didn't know how long the guards were supposed to wait. Or what they would do when they found he was the survivor...

But they couldn't ask about Dutch

because they weren't supposed to know he was here, on his killing mission. They couldn't give themselves away because Luckett would never let up until he had found out just what had happened, and how they had been corrupted.

High water!

The words swept into his mind. The woodyard was on the high side of the Gila River and it was high water, both rivers reaching up feet more than usual because of some disturbance way upstream, likely a flash flood or big snowmelt, that had swollen them.

The Gila was raging, chocolate-coloured thunder...

Even while these thoughts were racing through his head, Dallas gripped Dutch under the arms and dragged him across the yard to the fence along the river-bank. It was high and steep and no one ever seriously thought of it as a way of escape, simply because it wasn't. The river flowed into the Colorado but its course ran right along the boundary of the prison grounds, under the direct view of the wall guards.

A man trying to work the muddy, frothing waters stood a mighty big chance of being seen – if he didn't drown first. But that wouldn't bother Dutch Holland.

He somehow got the heavy man to the edge of the bank, slipped down to one knee, almost losing his grip and going over the edge into the roaring waters below. But he managed to strain backwards and hold on a little longer, working Dutch into the position he wanted. He yanked the knife out, decided it would be too incriminating to keep and tossed it far out. He didn't see where it fell into the river: the surface was too rough and disturbed for that.

Next, with a supreme effort, he managed to lift Dutch's body above his head and he heaved it out, once again almost going after it himself. He grabbed the crumbling edge, crawled back, his side bleeding copiously now.

Dizzy from his efforts, he returned to the

woodyard and picked up his axe just as Scottie and his companion guard started through the gate, herding in their prisoners. Both men stopped and stared at Dallas and he waved his axe.

'Cut myself,' he panted. 'Might have to see the doc...'

The prisoners filed in, all watching him closely, and he knew all but the greenhorns had known Dutch was going to make his try for him today. The guards had been fixed to make sure he was left alone with him.

Scottie walked across slowly, rifle at the ready, staring warily. He looked at the fresh mud on Dallas's trousers.

'Yeah – looks like you better see the sawbones, I guess. Tell him you cut yourself on your axe – he'll believe that. But might be best not to try to explain too much – savvy?'

'I'll explain things satisfactorily, don't worry.'

'*I* ain't worried.' But he didn't sound too confident. 'But mebbe you should worry – if you start tellin' lies about what happened.'

'Now why would I do that? I *know* what happened. I guess I'm not likely to forget it, either.'

Scottie paled, but growled a muttered threat, barely heard, then turned away, shaking his head at the other guard who was looking about him, obviously wondering where Dutch Holland was. Then suddenly Todd Yancey was beside Dallas, awkwardly trying to split a block of wood, while Dallas gathered up his shirt and hat to take with him to the doctor's.

'Reckon you and me are gonna be real good friends from now on, Dallas. If you're smart, it ought to work out just fine for both of us... OK?'

Dallas said nothing as he limped towards the woodyard gate.

What the hell was the kid talking about?

5

'Turn Him Loose!'

Warden Nathan Luckett was a blocky man, looked as wide as he was tall, but had an overpowering presence wherever he was.

Right now, he was in his office, behind his desk, elbows resting on the edge as he looked up at Frank Dallas standing between two armed guards.

'Holland's body was seen floating past on the current, Dallas.' Luckett's voice was deep and although at a reasonable level, seemed to have some kind of menace in it. Maybe it was the steely glint to his eyes that added to the impression. 'Three different wall guards identified the body drifting by. The only place he could've entered the river unseen was at the high-water cove behind the woodyard.'

'Yessir,' Dallas said, figuring he ought to say something. 'Recover the body, sir?'

Luckett's eyes slitted. 'No. Water's running far too fast – but don't you worry about that part. Here's your worry, Dallas – my investigations show that you were left alone in the woodyard at about the time Holland must have entered the river. There'll be some trouble for Scott and Foran for allowing the prisoners an unscheduled 'break', have no fear about that ... what I want to know is what happened between you and Holland.'

'Nothing happened, Warden. Foran told me to stay behind and catch up on my quota. I'd – er – sprained my wrist and couldn't use an axe as well as usual. I just went on cutting until Scott and Foran brought the men back. Including the greenhorns. I know nothing about Dutch.'

Luckett continued to drill his gaze into the prisoner. 'That's all you have to say?'

'Yessir – I'd tell you more if I could.'

Luckett almost smiled. 'I'm sure you would,' he said sardonically. 'Well, I've dealt with enough prisoners to know it'd be a waste of time waiting for you to admit to having fought with Holland and...'

'No, *sir! No fight.*'

'Be quiet! I'm not a fool, Dallas. Holland was a pain in my butt and had been for a long time. I'm glad he's gone. The rest of his crew will be scattered amongst other prisons and chain-gangs. Might as well clean out the whole nest of rats while I'm about it. But you're a different matter. Mostly you don't make trouble, but I wouldn't want you to think that you can get away with murder twice in my jail. Oh, don't frown like that. I have my sources and I know how Fizz McMasters came to swallow that mud.'

Dallas remained silent, waiting for his punishment to be announced. It was just seconds coming.

'I'd like you to think about your life in here Dallas, how it's been up until now, how it may be from now on. So I'm going to give you time to do that thinking.' He flicked his eyes to the guards. 'Two weeks in the Dark Cell – and on your way out, send in Scott and Foran.'

The guards took Dallas by the arms and hustled him out. Scott and Foran sat hunched over in chairs in the outer office, pale faces drawn and grey, awaiting their turn, cursing the day they had been tempted by Holland's bribe and tried to outwit Warden Nathan Luckett.

The three men came around the corner of the big, white two-storey frame house and stopped in their tracks, staring. It was an unusual sight right enough.

Judge Vernon Samuels was down on his hands and knees, being 'ridden' by a gurgling baby held on his broad back by a woman with deep red hair and a milk-white skin. She, too, was laughing as the judge neighed like a horse and even gave a small buck that lifted the baby slightly.

The men chuckled and looked at each other, highly amused and not trying to hide it.

Then the woman saw them and immediately snatched the baby to her bosom, saying sharply, 'Father! We have visitors!'

The judge stopped his cantering about instantly, snapped up his head and saw the men grinning at him.

'You make a fine hoss, Judge!' chuckled Solomon Yancey. 'Bet I could ride you to a standstill, though – without even using my spurs.'

Bo Kirby grinned widely while the other man, wearing a claw-hammer coat over pale-grey vest and white shirt with a blackstring tie, smiled thinly. He had a narrow, hawk-like face, and gripped a gold-handled walking cane as the judge scrambled to his feet with a grunt, dusting off his hands, face colouring a deep red.

Yancey walked forward, hand out-thrust. 'Solomon Yancey, Judge, from the Muggyown. I'm here to–'

'I can guess why you're here, Yancey,' cut in Samuels, curtly, ignoring the proffered hand. 'If you want to see me about any legal matters, you come to my chambers behind the courthouse in the morning.'

'This won't wait till mornin', Judge!' Yancey snapped, eyes narrowing. 'I want to–'

'You're trespassing, all three of you,' Samuels interrupted rudely, fixing his gaze on the man in the claw-hammer coat now. 'You know that's so, Ball. I can make it stick if I want to – and I want to. You and your client can see me tomorrow morning at ten in my chambers in town.'

Roderick Ball, attorney-at-law, tightened his thin lips and looked at Yancey. 'It's best we avoid any hostile confrontations, Sol. We can do this better in the judge's rooms, anyway.'

Bo Kirby hooked his thumbs in his gunbelt and looked arrogantly at Samuels' red-haired daughter as she hushed the baby who was crying for more rides on his grandfather's back, reaching out tiny arms towards the judge.

'All right,' the rancher said sullenly, glaring. 'But we get right down to tin-tacks tomorrer, Samuels. *Right* down!'

The trio turned and started back around the corner of the house, Kirby pausing to smile at the woman. 'Nice baby,' he said, touching the brim of his hat lightly.

She tightened her grip on the child as the gunman followed his boss and the lawyer around the corner.

Judge Samuels frowned. 'Those three are going to make me a lot of trouble. I can feel it.'

But the judge was ready for them when they entered his office the next morning when, without preamble, Sol Yancey said, 'I want my son turned loose from Yuma.'

'Come back in ten years' time – although a miracle may happen and he could be paroled before then.' The judge spoke shortly, unafraid of the three.

Kirby leaned against the door as if to prevent anyone entering. Ball and Yancey took chairs in front of Samuels' desk. The cattleman leaned forward.

'Look, Samuels, you know Todd ain't responsible.' He snapped his fingers at Ball who produced some papers from his valise and handed one to Yancey. 'I have here an affidavit from Dr Charles Udall, San Francisco. I took the boy to him for treatment once and he wrote this out for me to show if ever Todd got himself into trouble.'

'Which he seems to do with monotonous regularity,' allowed Samuels, taking the paper Yancey handed him. He scanned it quickly. 'Says the boy suffers from blackouts, has no recollection of what he does while he's in this blanked-out state... It's a good defence, I admit, but carries no weight with me.

Solomon Yancey's square jaw dropped. Roderick Ball frowned. 'That's a legally-attested document signed by an eminent physician, Judge!' Ball said. 'No court in the land would dispute that.'

'Perhaps not. But it doesn't mean I have to believe it.'

Ball quickly placed a hand on Yancey's forearm as the rancher started to rise. 'You – er – have medical qualifications we don't know about, Judge?' Ball asked, barely hiding his sneer.

Samuels flipped the paper across his desk. It balanced on the front edge, poised a moment and then began to fall. Ball snatched it instinctively.

'Those affidavits can be bought, Counsellor, you know that as well as I do.'

'Now, see here, Judge! I'm not going to stand for that!'

'Then leave,' Samuels told him, although he was staring at Sol Yancey whose jaw was knotted with muscle it was clamped so tightly. 'Yancey, everyone knows it costs you a small fortune to keep that kid of yours in line. That paper may or may not get him off the hook in certain circumstances; it means nothing to me. You bring this Dr Udall out from 'Frisco, stand him in front of my desk – *and* a panel of medical experts which I will assemble – and if he can convince all of us that what he says about your son's blackouts is true, then I'll reconsider his case.'

Yancey eased back in his chair, remained silent for a long minute. 'S'pose I spent a little bit of that "small fortune" you was talkin' about in this town, Judge? I mean, I seen your church on the way in and it'd look right nice with a steeple ... or maybe your school buildin' could stand a mite of attention...' He spread his hands. 'You'd know better'n me just what's needed. Mebbe somethin' a little closer to home? I dunno. So you tell me and I'll see that it's done. I'm always civic-minded, right, Rod?'

Ball flushed. 'Sol, I don't think this is the place for that kind of approach...'

'Sure it is. The judge'd like to have the town pat him on the back for gettin' the church a new steeple or some such – right, Judge?'

Samuels sighed, staring hard at Yancey.

'You're as rough round the edges as I've heard, Yancey. Consider yourself lucky I don't slap an attempted bribery charge on you.'

'Aw, now, Judge,' protested Ball immediately. 'You know that's not necessary. Why, Mr Yancey was simply trying to find a way to keep everyone happy. He's concerned about his son and rightly so, just as any father would be. So, if there's something else you'd like us to do that may or may not secure the release of young Todd, why, we'll be happy to listen to you – Sol?'

His blue eyes flashed a warning at the tight-lipped rancher and Yancey drew in a deep breath and nodded curtly.

'Sure. Just name it, Judge.'

Samuels shook his head slowly. 'You're both being dense, so I'll say it in words of one syllable that even your gunfighter holding up my door ought to be able to understand.'

Bo Kirby's face tightened, but he didn't move.

'Todd Yancey caused the death of three people, and the fire he started injured eleven others. In my opinion, he ought to hang, but I've been lenient – don't ask me why – and certainly don't *ever* again ask me to turn him loose before his ten-year sentence is up.'

Yancey glared at the attorney, throwing the ball into his court. Roderick Ball cleared his throat.

'Judge, they say you go by the book, but it isn't the book approved by Congress. You ask me, it appears to be one you've written yourself.'

Judge Samuels surprised them by smiling faintly. 'It's the same book, Counsellor, it's just that I've adapted it to frontier use, put my own interpretation on it, if you like, and, yes, I admit, I may have changed the rules a little, but I always act within the spirit of the law, if not the exact letter.'

Ball's smile was tight and without much humour now.

'I believe I could get a retrial on what I

know of young Todd's sentencing, Judge. Could your reputation stand that?'

Samuels' eyes narrowed and then that cold smile touched his lips and he spread his hands. 'I believe I could survive, Counsellor. Why don't you put it to the test?'

Samuels stood abruptly, soberly, without giving Ball a chance to reply.

'Now, good morning to you, gentlemen. I have the day's court business to attend to and you've kept me late already.' He raised his voice. *'Sheriff!'*

Bo Kirby staggered forward as the heavy door behind him opened and caught him in the back. He stumbled and came out of his crouch with his hand hovering above his gun butt. But he made no other movement as Big Arch Lake came in, sawn-off shotgun held loosely in his hands. He wore Dallas's stag-handled Colt on his hip. 'Ready now, Judge?'

'That I am, Arch,' Samuels said, stepping out from behind his desk and nodding farewell to the trio.

As he passed Sol Yancey, the rancher

grabbed the judge by the arm, leaned his head close.

'Turn him loose, Samuels!'

That was all. He didn't need to threaten the judge who pulled his arm free irritably and turned to face Yancey.

'Don't you or any of your lackeys ever – *ever* – come to my home again! Or you'll be able to talk face to face with your son – and tell him how you failed to secure his release. I'm ready now, Sheriff. I'll go on ahead. You'll see that these men leave the premises...?'

'Be my pleasure, Judge, be my pleasure.'

It must be like being dead, Dallas decided, sitting against the cold, rough stone wall in the Dark Cell.

There was just – nothing.

Nothing to see; nothing to hear – except his own ragged breathing and, occasionally, the thudding of his heart. Nothing to eat till sundown; nothing to do but sit here and think and rot.

He had had three – or was it four? – meals, so that meant he had been here three – or four – days so far.

'Goddamnit,' he said aloud, just to hear something. 'Was it three or four meals? Figure it out, give you something to do.'

So he set about trying to remember. Trouble was, each meal was the same tasteless, mostly cold mush.

If he had been able to say that the first meal had potatoes in it, the second carrots, the third meat, he might have been able to count with some certainty, but this way there was only frustration and he swore aloud, his own voice ramming back at him from the unseen walls.

He got a hold of himself, smelling the stale sweat of his aching body. Take it easy, feller! Three – or four – days and you start to yell at the blackness.

At the nothing...

By the end of the first week, you'll be gibbering, so get a hold of yourself, a *damn good hold!*

He took deep breaths, felt his pulse slow, the spread of calm from just below the arch of his ribs.

That was better. Think about something else, something outside of this place, travel far and well. You've got a mind, so you can do that.

Leave this hell-hole for a while.

Long years in prison had taught him that the only way to survive this 'solitary' was to project his mind a long way from here ... a long, long way from here.

After a while it seemed to work and he was no longer aware of the cell and his isolation.

6

Protector

Todd Yancey was worried. In the midst of all the other prisoners, he felt very much alone.

His father and the attorney, Ball, had been to visit, allowed ten minutes by a reluctant Warden Luckett, but they had no good news for him.

'That goddamn judge is as stubborn as all get-out,' growled Solomon Yancey. 'Tried everythin', bribes, veiled threats; Ball here even claimed there was a good case to have the judge disbarred because of the way he was runnin' his court, but all the son of a bitch did was grin and tell him to go ahead and try.'

'I think he knew I was bluffing, Sol,' Ball said quietly. 'I haven't really got anything that could have him disbarred.'

Yancey Senior had rounded on the startled attorney, speaking through gritted teeth. 'Then damn well *find* somethin'! I'm payin' you enough as a retainer and you make plenty off me in other ways, so you start earnin' your money, mister! I want Todd outa here quick as can be!'

Roderick Ball heaved a sigh. 'Sol, I'm doing all I can now within the letter of the law and–'

'Step *outside* the damn law then!' Yancey cut in savagely. 'Do *anythin'* you have to, but do *somethin' and fast!*'

Ball shook his head slightly. 'I can't break the law, Sol, you know that...'

'If there's no other way, you *break* it!' Yancey turned back to the silent Todd. 'Luckett won't let me do much for you, says it only starts envy amongst the other prisoners to see one of their kind gettin' special treatment, but I've left some money you can use for better grub or warmer clothes ... but don't worry, I'll have you outa

103

here soon.' He swivelled his cold gaze to the lawyer. 'Or I'll damn well know the reason why.'

That was about the end of the visit and Todd hadn't seen or heard from his father since. But the word had spread that he was able to buy 'special' items and better food.

So, the next morning, coming out of the latrines, he was stopped by Skip Hart and three more of the late unlamented Dutch Holland's bunch.

Word was they were awaiting transfer out to other jails as soon as they could be slotted in, but meantime they were ruling the roost in the Yuma prison yard in Holland's place.

Todd felt his bowels quake at sight of the hardcases, catching the glint of light from home-made knives and brass knuckles as Skip Hart stepped forward.

Skip was lean and mean, a rawhide length of muscle and sinew with absolutely no feelings at all for any other human being. He was ugly to look at and had many missing teeth from past brawls.

'Howdy, kid. Time we got acquainted, huh?'

Todd swallowed. He wasn't a coward, but he already knew the reputation of this gang and saw in a single sweeping glance that he was totally alone. 'I – know who you are.'

Skip turned to his men and nodded, with a 'Now ain't that somethin'' kind of look. 'Well, you'll know that anyone who's allowed outside funds has to pay a percentage to us.'

'N-no, I didn't know that.'

'Oh, yeah, been that way for a long time – goin' rate's fifty per cent.'

'Like hell!'

Skip grinned showing his gapped and broken teeth, holding up a hand, looking calm and relaxed. 'Now, before you start gettin' all fussed ... fifty per cent is what it is. We have to ... persuade you to pay up, it goes up to sixty. We have to do some more persuadin' and it's seventy – well, you get the picture. The longer you hold out, the more you gotta pay in the long run. Some fellers've been known to die and we get all the money anyways – so fifty per cent's a pretty fair price, kid. You think it over, tell us tomorrer – and have your money handy. Then you can ask Pappy for more!'

Skip stepped back and the other three moved in, one getting behind Todd so he couldn't retreat.

'Just to help you make a good decision,' Skip Hart said, rolling a cigarette as his men closed in on Yancey.

They didn't use the knives, except to rip some holes in Todd's warm jacket, but a couple of the blows he took in the ribs had the added weight of brass knuckles slamming against his flesh. They worked on his body mainly, so the marks of a beating wouldn't show on his face. He slid down, his feeble attempts at protection absolutely useless against these pros.

The boots beat a tattoo on his body from ankles to armpits, and he was left lying in the slush of the latrine building, moaning, coughing, tasting blood in the back of his throat, hoping none of his injured ribs had penetrated a lung. But Skip's crew were too professional for that. He was hurt and he would feel that hurt for days to come but he dragged himself outside and, later in the morning, contrived a fall down a low part of the quarry face so he could be taken to the infirmary where he was patched up.

'I believe I've been working within the prison system long enough to recognize the signs of a beating, son,' the amiable doctor said, as he bandaged his ribs. 'If you want to see the warden, I can arrange it.'

'No!' Todd gasped quickly. 'I fell down the quarry. Ask anyone on the work detail.'

'Of course ... but take my advice, son, you'd get a kinder reception from Warden Luckett if you were sent to him by me, than if you were caught brawling and had to be dragged before him by the guards...'

Todd refused to say any more, but when he was sent back to work that afternoon he wished he had listened to the doctor.

Skip Hart managed to pass close by him

and said, 'Nice stunt, kid, but if you don't cough up tomorrow, you'll never make the infirmary on your own two feet. After that, it only gets worse... Think about it tonight.'

Todd did – and he was afraid of another beating. His ribs wouldn't take much more without splintering and he'd seen a man die from punctured lungs once and hadn't liked it at all.

But it wasn't just the money he would have to pay over so as to avoid another beating: he knew Skip, or someone who would take his place, would work on him for as long as he was here, beating-up on him, bending him to their will, bleeding him of every cent his father managed to give him...

Todd Yancey didn't like pain and suffering. Leastways, not for himself. He had no feelings about other folk upon whom he might have inflicted such things.

He was being watched closely by Skip's crew and knew they were just waiting their chance to corner him and see if he was going to show some sense and pay their fifty per cent. There was no chance he could get to the infirmary and get the doctor's referral to the warden.

There was only one other way he could get to see Luckett and his stomach churned at the thought, but then he acted immediately, before he could worry too much about it.

As the guard, a man called Raven, passed on his patrol of the working party, Todd Yancey deliberately swung his pick handle across the man's shins, tripping him up. Raven yelled and stumbled and Yancey rammed his shoulder into the man, putting him down in the slush of the blue claybank adjoining the quarry and threw himself clumsily across the man, shouting, 'I'm not taking any more of your pushing around, damn you!'

Raven struck out with his rifle butt, cracking it across Todd's head. He managed to twist partly aside, fell awkwardly and the guard growled as he got to his feet and kicked him in the stomach. Other guards had come running and Raven swore, yanked the dazed Yancey upright.

'You crazy goddamn asshole! The hell'd you do that for?'

Yancey spat on the man's uniform jacket and there was an explosion of stars behind his eyes.

Just before he passed out all the way, he heard Raven say, 'Gimme a hand to get this stupid sonuver up to the warden for punishment!' – and he also glimpsed the furious face of Skip Hart before blackness swept over him.

He sat in a chair in the warden's office while Luckett heard about the incident from Raven and two other guards who had witnessed the unprovoked attack.

'What have you to say, Yancey?' Luckett snapped.

'Quite a lot, Warden,' Todd replied, jerking his throbbing head towards the guards. 'A lot more than my reason for jumping Mr Raven, sir ... but it's kind of private.'

Luckett's eyes narrowed. 'Are you saying you staged this attack just so you'd be brought before me?'

'I am, sir – otherwise, there were certain men who would've seen to it that I had another "accident" – quite a serious one this time. I'm prepared to name names, and I can also tell you what really happened to Dutch Holland...'

Luckett glared, indecisively.

Frank Dallas had lost all notion of passing time since they had flung him into the Dark Cell but he knew that the two weeks he had been sentenced to couldn't possibly be up when the door was crashed open and a guard told him to come on out. He flung an arm across his eyes to protect them from the blinding glare.

'What's up?' he asked hoarsely.

A rough hand gripped his arm, hauled him to his feet and flung him out through the doorway. He sprawled on hands and knees, grunting.

'Git on across to the latrines and clean yourself up – warden wants to see you...'

Dallas was still bewildered when, looking slightly cleaner in fresh prison clothes, although still barefoot, he was ushered into Luckett's office. The warden gestured to a chair and told the guard to wait outside the door.

When the man had gone, Luckett leaned back in his chair, staring hard and long and silently at Dallas. The gunfighter remained quiet, hands clasped in his lap.

'So Dutch tried to knife you because of what you did to Fizz McMasters, only you got the better of him and dumped his body in the river outside the woodyard fence.'

Dallas had a hard time keeping his face straight. *How could anyone know that? He and Dutch had been alone, the gates closed ... no one could have seen what happened!*

'You had a witness you didn't know about, Dallas,' Luckett told him quietly. 'Saw the whole thing, has described it to me blow by blow, several times – and each time it has been exactly the same. I believe him – and it is, after all, the most logical explanation. I suspected something like that, but knew you would never admit to it.'

He waited and still Dallas said nothing. Luckett showed signs of anger.

'Don't be a fool, Dallas! You know I'm not lying about the witness. Would you like me to describe how you ran along one of the dead trees destined for firewood, getting above Dutch, and then jumped down on him? Or how you snapped his wrist in your efforts to get the knife from him?'

By hell, someone had *seen the whole thing!*

Aloud, Dallas said, 'No, sir, I reckon there was a witness, but damned if I know where he could've been.'

Luckett almost smiled. 'He was hiding amongst the pile of dead trees, getting out of a little work...'

Dallas frowned. 'But the guards would've missed him when they herded the others out.'

'Not a newly arrived prisoner, just one amongst a whole bunch of new arrivals, all with shaven heads and prison uniforms ...

be easy to slip up.'

Dallas nodded, flicking his eyes to Luckett's hard face. 'Figured I'd only get another six months or more tacked on to my sentence, if I told about it, Warden.'

'Not to mention the unspoken code of the inmates, eh? Never spill the beans on a brother convict.'

Dallas shrugged. 'I was thinking of myself, sir. Dutch was dead, and I didn't give a damn about Skip and the rest. Still don't.'

'No – well, they'll be shipped out pretty soon, anyway. It was a clear case of self-defence and so the remainder of your sentence in the Dark Cell has been rescinded – you can return to the woodyard. Or would you rather I placed you somewhere else?'

Dallas held the man's unwavering stare. 'One place is as good as another, Warden.'

'I suppose it is. Hart and his men will do time in the Dark Cell until I can place them at another prison. You haven't yet asked who was the informant who came forward and got you off the hook, Dallas.'

'I can figure out who it must've been, Warden.'

'Very well...' He seemed to hesitate, then said, sounding puzzled, 'I really don't know for sure why the man in question *did* come forward. Part of it was to get himself out of trouble with Hart's gang, but the rest – I'm not sure. But just let me warn you, if there is some reason behind it that I can't see just now, and it involves an escape attempt or–'

'Warden, I've been to every part of this prison and I've thought about escape ever since I came here. A long time back, I decided the only sure way out of Yuma is to serve out your time – or die and be buried up on Cemetery Hill.'

Luckett nodded. 'Glad to know you have that much sense, Dallas.'

'Doesn't mean I won't still try to figure something, though, Warden.'

Luckett's face clamped shut abruptly. 'Don't get smart-ass with me, Dallas! *Guard!* Take this man back to the quarry and put him on full quota – and keep an eye on him and whoever he associates with... I want daily reports.'

Todd Yancey was working at the blue clay-bank adjacent to the quarry, slowly and stiffly because of the beating he had taken.

He was a lot happier, though, knowing Skip Hart and his crew were locked in the blackness of the Dark Cell area.

Dallas came past from time to time, wheeling broken rock and dumping it on the workpile near the claybank where mountains of the strange bluish-hued clay were building.

Yancey contrived to be at the mound of clay, emptying a wooden barrowload, at the same time as Dallas.

'Better out here than in the Dark Cell, eh?'

Dallas didn't look at him, aware that he must be being watched. When he spoke, his lips barely moved.

'Much better. Obliged for you speaking up. You could've gotten punishment yourself, hiding from the work party that way.'

'Ah, I'm a pretty good judge of men. I knew Luckett wouldn't do that to me.'

'But he's curious as to why – just like I am.'

'Yeah?' Todd Yancey sounded genuinely surprised. 'Hell, I thought it'd be obvious to you...'

Guards were coming across and Dallas hefted the now empty barrow, turned and started back towards the quarry section.

He had taken perhaps a dozen steps when Yancey said quietly, but clearly, 'I need a protector, Dallas! And you're him!'

7

Hard Man

So that was the price he had to pay for Yancey getting him out of the Dark Cell.

OK, Dallas thought. Fair enough.

And it wasn't long before he was called upon to give Yancey 'protection'.

Skip Hart and his pards were no longer a threat: they would stay in the Dark Cell until they were shipped out to other jails, but there were others who wanted to step into the shoes of Dutch Holland. A man called Hotchner had designs on being the new kingpin of Yuma Pen and he had hardcases to back him but, being large and brutal, he took on Todd Yancey alone. It was not an even match, but Hotch, as his friends called him, didn't care about that.

He cornered the kid behind a pile of rubble in the quarry, fisted up the kid's jacket and lifted him easily clear of the ground.

'I hear your old man's due to send you some more money ... bring it straight to me, OK?'

Hotch's breath was like the wrong end of a buffalo and spittle flew when he spoke with his heavy lips. Yancey turned his head away, grimacing. But he looked back sharply at the man's words, eyes widening.

'*All* of it?'

Hotch slammed him back against the pile of rock. Yancey moaned, afraid his spine was broken. 'You ain't hard of hearin'! You know what I said. You bring it straight to me. No one else – an' just so you don't forget...'

Hotch grunted with effort and literally threw the kid high up the pile and Yancey sprawled on the broken rock, feeling it bite into his body. As he tumbled back down, Hotch lifted a big splayed foot and stomped him in the belly. He walked away, leaving the kid curled up on the muddy ground, retching, bleeding...

In the mess hall later, Yancey found a seat next to Dallas on the hard form at the plank tables. Dallas was eating his soup mechanically, breaking the hard, dark rye bread and softening it in the lukewarm liquid before stuffing it into his mouth.

After a while he became aware that the kid wasn't eating, only stirring the soup. 'Get it into you, kid, it'll warm you up before you go back to the quarry.'

Yancey pushed his tin bowl of soup across to Dallas. 'You can have it – I wouldn't be able to keep it down.'

Dallas arched his eyebrows. 'Stomach upset?'

'Yeah! Upset by a size fourteen foot that belongs to Hotchner! Liked to kick my belly out through my spine, the bastard!'

Dallas slowly lowered his spoon, looking levelly at Yancey. The kid leaned closer, told him how Hotchner had waylaid him behind the rubble pile.

'I never felt strength like it,' the kid finished, rubbing his sore stomach gently. 'My back's all cut, and so's the back of my head. Man, he *threw* me six feet straight up!'

Dallas was sober now and spoke quietly. 'When is your father s'posed to bring your money?'

'Tomorrow. If he leaves it, I have to give it to Hotch. If I don't take it, Hotch'll kill me.' Yancey gave a crooked smile. 'Unless you'd like to talk Hotch out of it?'

'That what you want me to do?'

Yancey shrugged. 'You *are* supposed to be my protector. I mean, I got you out of the Dark Cell...'

'I don't forget my obligations, kid – OK. Hotch won't bother you. You take whatever money your father gives you. I won't let Hotch take it from you.'

'You mean it? Hotch is a lot bigger than Dutch, but he's not so smart.'

'I'll take care of it,' Dallas said and the kid knew it was a promise.

He sat back, smiling, pulling his bowl of

soup towards him, his appetite suddenly having revived.

Dallas figured a man like Hotchner wouldn't bother to have back-up when he braced the kid for the money. It would be a come-down in Hotch's eyes: he had given the kid his orders, now all he had to do was collect. It would be more prestige if he did it alone – and he figured it would be the easiest money he had ever made.

Dallas reckoned Hotch would jump the kid in the same place, away from the guards' normal patrol boundary, so he casually worked his own way towards the rubble pile and when Yancey returned from seeing his father and the kid gave him the nod, Dallas made sure it was clear before he slipped around the rubble pile.

He was in time to see Hotchner step out from behind a large heap of slate slabs and block the kid's path. Yancey stopped, and Dallas heard Hotch say, as he held out one large hand, 'Gimme.'

Yancey looked around to make sure Dallas was there and, although Dallas had told him to hand over the money – or something that could be mistaken for it – so as to divert Hotch's attention, the kid thrust his hands into his pockets and said, 'I don't think so, you pile of blubber! But you just discuss it with my bodyguard!'

Dallas cursed. Instead of being able to slip around behind Hotch while he was reaching for the money – or what he thought was the money – he was now alerted and caught Dallas flat-footed starting towards him.

Hotch frowned, his brain moving slowly, but then he swung a backhand blow that took Yancey across the side of the head and sent him tumbling and sprawling three yards away. By that time the giant Hotch was closing in on Dallas, thick, rubbery lips peeling back from big, stained teeth.

'Never liked you much, Dallas, anyway!' he growled, and reached for the gunfighter with arms like tree branches.

Dallas ducked and dodged to the side,

slipping in the mud. Hotch stumbled, but he was fast for a big man and one horny foot slapped against Dallas's head and sent him rolling. By the time he pushed to his feet, Hotch was moving in, ham-sized fists hammering. Dallas thought his head had been torn off his shoulders and he staggered wildly, fighting for balance. Hotch kicked his legs out from under him, stomped a foot at his spine.

Dallas twisted away, lights spinning and whirling behind his eyes, ears ringing from the head blow. Mud splashed into his face as the big foot missed him by inches. Then his hand closed over a piece of rock and he swung hard, bringing it down squarely on the grimy instep.

Something crunched and Hotch roared like a bear with a bellyache and hopped awkwardly, reaching for his mangled, bleeding foot.

Dallas didn't waste time. He lunged to his feet, kicked the man's supporting leg four times before it collapsed and Hotch went down. The big man was in agony but he scooped up a rock the size of a melon and hurled it at Dallas. It bounced off his shoulder and the gunfighter fell to his hands and knees. Hotch reached for him, managed to get a grip on his head and smashed Dallas's face down into the mud.

Hotch tried to hold him there, suffocating him, but he was just a little too far away to get that much leverage and, gagging, hawking, gasping, Dallas rolled free, pivoted on his throbbing shoulder and drove both feet into the big man's face.

Hotch's head snapped back and he instinctively tried to get up, put his weight on his crushed foot and again collapsed, howling. Dallas knew he had to end this – and *now!* He picked up another rock and hurled himself at Hotchner, slamming the rock against the hard head with all his weight behind it.

Hotch went down and stayed down, breathing with shuddering, snuffling sounds, blood pouring from the deep gash in his head...

Dallas crouched there, panting, fighting for breath, still holding the bloody rock. Then, he heaved to his feet, stumbled forward, lifted Hotch's legs and threw his weight backwards. He rolled the unconscious man in against the base of the rubble pile, then crawled part way up it and kicked at the loose rock until a large section slid down and partially covered Hotch. He laid the bloody rock near the man's head.

Hopefully it would look as if the rubble had shifted and fallen on the man.

Todd Yancey was on his feet, had been standing watching the fight. Now he grinned.

'Good work! You stick with me and you'll live pretty well while I'm around, Dallas!'

'Wait up, kid,' Dallas panted, blotting blood from his face and mouth with a dirty sleeve. He stumbled down to stand before the kid. 'That was it, Yancey, all there is.'

The kid frowned. 'What? All what is? What're you talking about?'

'You got me out of the Dark Cell; I saved your neck – now we're even.'

Dallas made to turn away but Yancey stepped forward, grabbed his arm hard, spinning him around, his face white. 'Hold up! You're my protector now! That's why I got you out of the Dark Cell! You owe me!'

Dallas shook his throbbing head gently. 'I just paid the debt, Yancey. You didn't save my life, only saved me a little inconvenience... I reckon we're square.'

'No! By God, we're not! I went out on a limb for you and you don't walk away from your obligations that easy, friend!'

'Kid, take your hand off my arm before I break it and stuff it down your throat. You're with the big boys now. Daddy's not here to get you out of every bit of trouble you get yourself into. Learn to stand on your own two feet, kid. I've done all I'm ever gonna do to help you ... just step easy from now on.'

Dallas pulled free and, rubbing his sore parts, made his way back to the work area.

Todd Yancey stood, white-faced, trembling, his mouth slack. But his mind was raging.

No one treated him that way! *No one!*

Solomon Yancey was going plumb loco, driven near crazy by the frustration of being unable to get Todd his freedom.

'That son of a bitch judge!' he spat, pacing his hotel room, watched by the deadpan Bo Kirby and the uncomfortable Roderick Ball. 'He could parole Todd any time!'

'Not quite true, Sol,' Ball said tentatively, and winced a little when Yancey flung his burning gaze at him. 'I mean, it's not all that easy; you can't *force* him to arrange a parole, it's a complicated process and–'

'Money will short cut *any* goddamned *complicated* process!' snapped the rancher. He paused and looked at Kirby who was lounging in a leather easy chair. 'And why ain't *you* doin' somethin' to earn what I pay you?'

Kirby shrugged. 'Tell me what you want

done and I'll do it.'

'Now hold up, Sol!' Ball said quickly. 'If you're going to be discussing anything even remotely less than legal here, I'm going. I can't stand by and be a party to anything that breaks the law.'

'Not unless the money's right, huh?' Sol said bitterly. 'You might's well go for all the good you've been.'

'Sol – my hands are tied. Judge Samuels has this neck of the woods sewn up. He's answerable to no one but himself. I can't find even a chink in his armour.'

'Like I said, you might as well go!'

Ball nodded, relieved, really, to be dismissed, but he thought he ought to show some reluctance and paused by the door. 'Isn't the boy being protected by this gunfighter he got out of solitary or something?'

Solomon Yancey curled a lip. 'Sonuver backed down. Sure, he got Todd outa some scrape but the kid's a target for every sewer rat servin' time in Yuma. This Dallas won't back him up no more.'

Ball hesitated, then said, 'Sol, I tried to tell you before: as long as you keep giving the boy money, someone will try to take it from him.'

Yancey's eyes bulged. 'You tellin' me I oughta let my boy eat that slop they call food, freeze his ass off in them threadbare prison clothes? Or under floursack blankets?'

'Of course not, but why not send him the things, the items, instead of giving him the cash? Someone might still try to take them, but if you make sure his name is all over them they'll soon be deterred. Warden Luckett is harsh on thieves within his prison.'

Yancey frowned, apparently calming down. 'You might have somethin' there ... all right. Go on. We'll meet for supper and see if you can come up with somethin' that'll get Todd outa there.'

As the attorney left, Bo Kirby cleared his throat and picked at his teeth with a matchstick sliver. 'Sol, there might be one way ... kinda desperate, but–'

'Let's hear it!' Yancey snapped. *'I'm* kinda desperate so it might be just what I want to hear.'

Frank Dallas saw the signs on the kid's face: bruising, swelling, dried blood crusted about his nostrils, and the stiff way he carried himself.

Todd Yancey had had yet another beating. The kid was a fool: instead of using the money his father smuggled into him wisely, he was trying to use it to buy power in the prison. After Dallas told him they were all squared away, the kid had tried to hire protection.

A couple of real hardcases had gone on his payroll and he figured he was safe now and sneered at Dallas when he passed by with his two 'protectors'. Next time Dallas saw him, the kid was nursing fresh injuries and had empty pockets.

His 'protectors' had simply beaten him up

themselves and taken his money. While he was broke, no one bothered with Todd Yancey; the day after Sol smuggled in more cash, the kid was beaten again.

He came to Dallas in the quarry yard, wheeling his shallow wooden barrow of lumps of blue clay cut from the claybank for an adobe wall the warden wanted built.

'You gotta help me!'

Dallas didn't look up, kept swinging his sledge as the kid emptied the clay near the plank-sided pit where the blue earth was being mixed with straw from a huge pile and eventually made into large bricks that would dry in the sun until hard before being used to build the adobe wall.

'Time you helped yourself, kid. You can't buy protection here. You've got to stand on your own two feet or they'll end up crippling you – may be worse.'

'You son of a bitch! *You owe me!*'

Dallas sighed, still didn't look up. 'Told you, kid, we're all square. Tell your old man to quit sending you money. They'll never leave you alone as long as you get cash in here.'

'They'd leave me alone if you stood up for me!'

'Kid, I'm doing time I reckon I oughtn't to have to do. I've looked over this place from top to bottom. There's no way out ... or only two ways: serve your time or die. I'm trying for parole, which means I have to stay outa trouble. I ain't gonna buy into yours ... sorry.'

'By hell, you *will* be!' Yancey hissed, starting off with his barrow. *'You damn well will be sorry!'*

Dallas kept swinging the sledge. But he didn't take the kid's petulant threat lightly. The kid was spoilt rotten, used to having his own way. When he was a child he likely smashed up any toy he couldn't have: that was his way.

So Dallas figured to tread warily from here on in. The kid could still buy his dirty work done...

Then, a couple of days later, Zack Ballard and Mohawk Magee came in with a new batch of prisoners and the kid greeted them like long-lost friends.

8

Riot!

If it hadn't been for the Mexican girl's jealousy, Zack and Mohawk might not have found Vinnie Cranston so quickly.

After his panic in Yuma when Todd Yancey had been charged with arson, Vinnie had run for the Border, slipped across and set himself up in the back of a ramshackle *cantina* in the small Mexican village of El Jubilo – though what there was to be jubilant about in such a backwoods cesspool was hard to see.

But Vinnie knew it would be a good hiding place and quickly endeared himself to a lady of the night who called herself Estrelita. She was, in fact, the star of the small bordello that the *cantina* owner ran in the back rooms of his establishment. The competition was not serious, but Estrelita was flattered when Vinnie took up more or less permanent residence in her rooms.

But one of the other lost doves was a younger girl called Conchita and she had large, liquid, dark eyes that did something to Vinnie's insides and generally turned the hardcase killer to mush. It took no time at all for Estrelita to figure out that something was going on and there was a big bust-up which resulted in Conchita having her face and one breast slashed and Vinnie Cranston a knife cut that stretched across his lower belly and almost into his groin.

In the confusion, Estrelita had escaped across the Border and made her way to Somerton, south of Yuma, where she heard that two Yankees were offering a fifty-dollar gold-piece for any information about another Yankee called Vinnie Cranston.

Within the hour the gold-piece was Estrelita's...

Then Zack Ballard and Mohawk Magee

made their way to the *cantina*, cracked a couple of heads and some stone jars of *pulque* before being directed to Vinnie's room. Zack kicked in the door while Mohawk went in crouching, gun in hand, surprising Vinnie trying to force himself on the mutilated Conchita in her bed.

He had rolled out, naked, groping for his gun on the chair, but Mohawk had smashed him across the head with his gun butt, kicked the man under the ear and stomped on his gun-hand for good measure. When people had come to see what the hysterical Conchita was screaming at now, Zack, feeling his head humming from the *pulque* he had drunk, shot two and then the Yankees had made their way out with the naked Vinnie thrown across Mohawk's wide shoulders.

They found clothes for him, beat him up on Solomon Yancey's behalf, dragged him behind a rope all the way back to Yuma. By then, Vinnie was really stove-up. The bandages on his belly had torn loose and he was half-dead from thirst.

Zack and Mohawk had brought liberated bottles of *tequila* from the *cantina* and were living in a half-drunk state. They grew lax and paid the penalty in a side street in South Yuma where a small crowd had gathered, watching them beat-up on Cranston.

Suddenly Vinnie came bouncing up out of the dirt, surprising them both. He punched Zack in the genitals and snatched the man's six-gun and began shooting immediately.

Mohawk dived for the dust, dropped his six-gun, but managed to get it in his hands as Vinnie roared and started running, scattering people. He half-turned and triggered at Mohawk who came up onto one knee, Colt bucking in his fist, the man barely able to see properly he was so drunk.

Someone cried out in pain. Glass shattered. A bullet ricocheted from an iron washtub hanging outside of a store window. People screamed and ran and still Mohawk kept shooting until the gun was empty.

By that time, two townsmen were down,

one lying very still in the dust and Vinnie Cranston was hanging onto an awning post of a hardware store, slowly sliding down, blood trickling from his mouth. He was dead by the time he hit the boardwalk. Then Sheriff Lake arrived with his shotgun...

It took hardly any time at all to convene a court and Judge Vernon Samuels ranted at the stupidity and irresponsibility of drunken trail bums thinking they could come into any town where he presided and start killing men and wounding citizens.

He sentenced both Zack and Mohawk to life imprisonment in Yuma Penitentiary...

Before they were sent out to the big prison, Solomon Yancey managed to visit Zack and Mohawk in the holding cell. They stared at their boss with crashing headaches and red eyes and Zack started right in apologizing for killing Vinnie.

They were surprised when Yancey nodded slowly. 'You did all right, boys. You found the son of a bitch and give him hell and now he's dead. But you're in bad trouble.'

'You gotta help us, Sol!' Mohawk said in his raspy voice. 'You gotta get us out before they send us to the Pen. Once inside we're there forever!'

'Can't be done, boys. I've tried, used my best man, Counsellor Ball himself, but that goddamned judge is bent on seein' you rot – 'cause you work for me is my guess.'

Zack sat down weakly, going greyish white. Mohawk's eyes bulged.

Sol lowered his voice, looked around at the dim passage and said, 'But, fellers, I'm here to tell you I got one thousand dollars for you – apiece that is – if you can stir things up in that prison and get Todd out in the confusion. An' yourselves, of course, at the same time.'

They blinked, not thinking fast enough to fully savvy what he was saying.

'How we gonna do that, Sol?'

'There's a guard, name of Black, who smuggles money and a few clothes in to Todd. You contact him when you get in there. You need anythin' to help you set things up, he'll get word to me. You want that money, boys?'

They wanted it all right but they were damned if they knew just what Solomon Yancey wanted in return – except in very general terms. He was leaving the details to them – and they saw it was their only chance of beating their life sentences.

They were duly taken to Yuma and passed into the prison population and when they saw young Todd, with the marks of his beatings, they knew they'd better blamed well come up with *something* – and fast – or old Sol would have their *cojones* for his dogs to play with.

Dallas didn't know Zack or Mohawk but he saw the way their arrival changed the kid.

He went from a worried, hunch-backed, jumpy inmate to one who laughed a mite too easily maybe, now, but he swaggered a bit, too – and there were no fresh bruises or cuts or other marks of beatings on him these days.

141

He guessed Zack and Mohawk were looking out for him and heard on the prison grapevine that a man who had 'borrowed' Todd Yancey's warm jacket sent in by his father had met with an accident. A bad one, too. It was said he might never walk again and was in some kind of a coma, so bad that the prison doctor had had him shipped out under escort to a proper hospital for care.

'One of the most brutal beatings – or should I say "most unfortunate *accidents*" that I've ever seen in my twenty-eight-year career,' the doctor confided in Dallas when he was getting a hand dressed after a rock had fallen on it.

There was a nurse there that day, one from the women's division who had to wait for one of her charges to recover from an anaesthetic after an emergency appendix operation. She was a nice-looking young woman, not beautiful, but she had a commanding face and a warm smile. If anything she was a little on the plump side, but fairly tall with it. What hair Dallas could see showing beneath the regulation mob-cap looked to be blonde. Her name was Jessica Gowan.

Now, tying-off the bandage around his wrist, she looked up sharply at the doctor's tone. 'Are you saying it wasn't an accident, Doctor?'

The medico smiled wearily. 'In this place, Jessica, I will believe nothing I'm told and half of what I see.'

She smiled that warm smile. 'Sounds like a very wise decision, Doctor.' She turned hazel eyes towards Dallas. 'Don't you think so?'

'Me?' Dallas arched his mud-spattered eyebrows, shook his head. 'I don't have any opinions, ma'am. Find I get along better by being just like the doc – keep my thoughts to myself.'

She laughed briefly, looking genuinely amused. 'I think you two worry-worts are trying to put me in my place!'

'Not guilty,' proclaimed the doctor, washing his hands.

'Me, neither, Nurse. But if you *needed* putting in your place, or whatever, I'd be happy to oblige.'

Her smile slowly faded and she frowned a little. The medico coughed lightly. 'Time for you to check your charge, I think, Jessica...'

Dallas's eyes followed her as she left the room.

'I don't need you any more, Dallas. Never did, really, but you were handy and I figured I could use you. Now, you're not even good enough for me to wipe my boots on.'

Todd Yancey made this short, bitter speech near the rockpile where, because of his sore hand, Dallas awkwardly dumped his barrowload of rock and the kid turned his high-sided barrow of clay into the slurry pit which was being worked desultorily by a couple of men.

Only when he glanced up at the kid's words, did Dallas recognize Zack and Mohawk. He tensed, but there didn't seem to be any immediate threat.

'Glad to hear it, kid. Now mebbe you'll leave me alone and I can get a little peace.'

Yancey smiled crookedly.

Over the next two weeks temperatures dropped and most prisoners turned inward on themselves, too blamed cold to be making small talk, keeping their eyes open for the smallest articles of clothing that could give them a mite of extra warmth. But Dallas really wasn't much worried by cold or heat or rain.

He was a man who had lived with and in the elements for so long that he had given up griping and beefing about any discomfort they caused. But colds and chest infections were rampant in the prison and the doctor was kept mighty busy, had to call on Jessica Gowan and her other two nursing-aid companions from the women's division to help out.

As for Todd Yancey, well, he had good warm clothes and blankets sent in by his father. It incited unrest among the other, less fortunate prisoners, and there were attempts to steal his 'goodies', but Zack Ballard and Mohawk Magee saw to it that he didn't lose any items.

Luckett did what he could, had asked the Prisons Department for extra blankets and warmer uniforms but nothing came of his requests. There was a growing lack of interest in Yuma now it was becoming established as an escape-proof prison: the department took the view that if this was so, then they could place prisoners there with confidence and forget about them. They couldn't go anywhere so give them minimum requirements and save public money.

As some form of concession, Luckett allowed the men to let their hair grow and to cultivate beards.

The rats were hungry, too, and prowled amongst the sleeping men in the dormitories. Bitter winds blew in from the rivers and the moaning they made winding their way through the dank passages and cells kept men awake, cursing.

And men lacking sleep were ill-tempered men, ready for anything that would change their lot for the better, even if there was only the slimmest chance of it succeeding.

The Yuma Penitentiary population was rife with dissension, ready for out-and-out revolt....

And Zack and Mohawk – and Todd Yancey, too – missed no opportunity to stir up their fellow inmates. There was an ugly mood within the walls of Yuma Prison, so much so that Warden Luckett had dispensed with his regular walks through the prison grounds to occasionally chat with his charges and see how work was progressing on various projects. He felt uneasy and didn't like the way some of the gaunt-faced creatures dressed in rags looked at him.

The doctor had cause to dress Dallas's leg one day for one of the many infected cuts suffered by all the men who worked in the quarry.

'Strange atmosphere in the prison of late, Mr Dallas,' the medico allowed.

Dallas looked at the man sharply. 'Just a lot of half-frozen men, Doc,' the gunfighter said crisply, wondering why he had avoided a direct answer.

He had seen men on the verge of revolt before, and in his opinion the inmates of Yuma were rapidly heading that way. All they needed was a leader, someone to light the fuse that would explode unrest into violence and death.

Three days later, the explosion occurred in Yuma.

Literally.

Later, Dallas figured that Solomon Yancey must have smuggled in the dynamite and fuses and blasting-caps inside innocent-looking parcels brought in by the corrupt guard named Black. Some of the items could even have been inside the lining of the warm clothing he had gotten to Todd.

The first charges went off early one frosty, mist-shrouded morning while the men stamped their feet and blew on their numbed hands in the breakfast line.

The very first blast was near the main gate, near enough to splinter some of the logs. The second was attached to a leg of the big water-tank just inside the gate – God alone knew how they had managed to plant *that!* – and the timber support splintered, buckled for a moment while the startled guards gripped the rails around the high walkway, clinging to the cold metal of the four-barrelled Lowell battery gun. In the end the whole kit-and-caboodle started its inevitable fall, albeit in slow motion. Two of the guards abandoned their post and leapt to the hard ground. Water dolloped out of the huge tank. The other two guards rode the tank down, but although jarred and hurled about violently, sustained no real injuries. Then the tank dumped its tons of gushing water in a miniature tidal wave, smashing one part of the heavy gate off its bottom hinge, making it jut out, leaving a space a desperate man might slip through.

Wrecking the guard tower had been an obvious attempt to put the deadly Lowell gun out of commission, but it was a complete failure.

As the breakfast line broke – Dallas was startled, along with a score of others who hadn't been taken into the conspiracy – and a roaring mob surged towards the flood and the splintered gate, aiming to force their way through the warped section, the two remaining guards picked themselves up and righted the heavy battery gun on its stand. They set it firmly on its iron legs and with easy expertise, readied it for firing, cocking, locking and loading swiftly.

Those in the very front of the mob saw what was happening, tried to stop the surge, but nothing short of an earthquake could have stopped that charge. The Lowell was a pretty good substitute, though, and the hammering blows as the quadruple barrels thundered, cut swathes in the ranks.

Bodies tumbled and were hurled spinning through the air, severed limbs and organs splattering back into the masses pushing from behind: it was like being hit at close range by the broadside from a ship of war.

There were more explosions and, later, Frank Dallas thought he counted six, but at the time wasn't aware of doing so. They came from the direction of the quarry. Smoke and debris were hurled into the chill morning air, masking the watery sun, giving the scene a look of twilight, a half-world filled with the screams and moans of demons from hell.

Dallas tangled with two men who tried to push him into the surge making for the gate, kicking one in the belly, head-butting another. He glimpsed their faces before they went down, glimpsed the madness there.

They were committed now, no matter what. And yet these men must have known before they had even agreed to join the revolt that it couldn't possibly succeed, though there *was* a slim chance that a few might make it. Even if they did, where could they go? Folk in Yuma would turn them in or shoot them down. South, there was the Border, but it was all open desert country that way and a man would either freeze, die of thirst or starvation, or be run down by the posses that would be out in force. Getting out didn't seem to be much of an option when you got right down to it.

Which didn't mean that Dallas wasn't going to try for freedom himself. He mightn't have been a part of the original plan but he *was* an opportunist, if nothing else, so he looked around, searching for signs of Zack and Mohawk – and the kid. They were the ones behind this: wherever they were lay the way out – if there *was* a way out.

The sites of the other explosions were a mystery to him: why would anyone set them off near the quarry and the blue claybank? There was no purpose to that, it was too far in from the river to be of any use, the cliffs behind the rock quarry were far too high to scale and if a man did manage to get to the top there was nowhere to go. So *why?* The answer was obvious – they were a diversion, designed to get the bewildered guards running towards the sound, leaving other parts of the prison grounds without adequate protection. *Which parts?* The main building, the infirmary, administration...?

By God, could they be crazy enough to try and take Luckett hostage! But, no, Luckett was a careful man and had his own personal bodyguard who would stick with him no matter what, once there was an emergency. Then who? The civilian clerks in the office who came in each day from Yuma town? Could be...

No! A more vulnerable place was the infirmary! The doctor was mighty popular and there were always nurses and women patients ... easy hostages.

'Judas! That's it!' he said aloud, and ducked instinctively as yet another charge blew, over towards the river fence of the woodyard. *Now* there was a chance for someone to get to the river, but only if a boat was waiting.

Anyone crazy enough to try to swim in those waters would freeze even before he had time to drown.

Dallas was starting towards the infirmary but changed his mind, ran back towards the woodyard through the powdersmoke and other fumes from fires lit by the rampaging convicts as they realized they weren't going anywhere. So they took out their frustrations by wreaking as much havoc as possible. Then the Lowell began hammering men to bloody rags around the gates again. Hopes were fading rapidly.

Dallas saw a guard coming towards him, yelling, lifting his rifle. The gunfighter leaned down without pausing and scooped up a handful of shattered rock, hurled it at the man. The rifle crashed but the guard instinctively tried to dodge the missiles coming at him and his aim was way off. By then Dallas was upon him. He wrenched the lever-action from the man's hands, quickly drove the brass-bound butt against the capped head. The guard sprawled and Dallas leapt over him, making for the woodyard.

Two of the stacks of cut timber billets were afire blazing high, filling the place with smoke. He dodged through half-crazed prisoners, slamming one in the belly as he tried to grab the rifle. Another sought to bring him down by wrapping his arms about his legs. Dallas coldly drove the carbine's butt down between his eyes.

The smoke was a good cover and he saw shadowy forms moving out at the edge by the fence. Coughing, he crouched low, able to see more clearly now even though his eyes stung.

He had been right and he had been wrong. They had made for the infirmary all right, but hadn't taken the doctor hostage: instead, they had dragged a couple of ailing female patients out of their sickbeds and used them as shields and hostages.

Then he glimpsed a flash of wheat-coloured hair, a roundish face as the mouth opened to scream in protest.

Nurse Jessica Gowan, running at the shadows.

Beyond her, he saw three men: Todd Yancey, Zack Ballard, and Mohawk Magee.

They all had knives and each held a female patient, except for Todd Yancey: he grabbed Nurse Gowan as she tried to free one of the sick women, pulled her in front of him and laid the knife blade against her throat.

He spun as Dallas's hazy figure came out of the smoke, mistaking him for a guard because he held a firearm.

'Take just one more step, mister, and I'll slit her from ear to ear!'

Jessica was struggling, but went very still at the crazed sound of Todd's voice.

'That ain't a guard, Todd!' croaked Mohawk, the smoke making his normally raspy voice even raspier. 'It's Dallas!'

Mohawk lifted his knife in a throwing movement and Dallas dropped to one knee, shot him through the chest, the man spinning away from his hostage who fell, sobbing. Zack Ballard made a lunge for Dallas who swung the carbine, levering, shot him through the left hip. Zack went down screaming, clutching his wound, writhing in his agony.

On the river, Dallas glimpsed two rowing boats, and the men in them started shooting with six-guns. Todd yelled.

'Watch it, you stupid bastards! I'm coming down!' He turned a wild-eyed face to Dallas, pulling Jessica in front of him again. 'Hey, Dallas – you want her?'

He slashed with the knife and the girl screamed as he flung her from him towards Dallas who lifted the rifle and blew the kid off his feet, his body sliding and tumbling down the slope to sprawl at the edge of the freezing river, face down in the mud.

Behind him, he heard heavy, running footsteps and Luckett's voice bellowing for him to drop the rifle or be shot where he stood.

Dallas let the gun fall.

9

Judgement Day

Seventeen men died in the attempted mass breakout and riot.

Two were guards (another four were badly wounded, two not expected to survive) and one was an administration worker, another a nurse and the rest were prisoners. Two would-be rescuers in the boats were also wounded, but they got away with all the boat crews. A search was proceeding.

There would be a huge line-up awaiting Judge Vernon Samuels to pass judgement on and Warden Luckett, not ordinarily a callous man, locked *all* inmates in their cells with only bread and water for sustenance during a week of the coldest days so far this winter.

So cold in fact that Judge Samuels would not venture out of his house as he already had a head cold and he had sent his daughter and grandson to a suite in the La Grande hotel in town. He did not want to risk the small child catching his cold as two babies in town had died within three days from chest infections that had started with head colds.

Meantime, the inmates shivered and starved and Luckett gave orders to hose them down with cold well water if there were any more signs of unrest.

Then came the day when they were turned out of their cells into crisp winter sunshine and were hosed down anyway because of their body stench. They were separated into groups: Group A included the worst offenders, men who had killed or maimed during the riot and had been named by guards who had witnessed their acts of brutality. Group B were those who had tagged along because they had little choice and had given up without trouble when cornered by the guards. Group C were those who had been wounded but could still walk around and their part in the riot was still to be determined.

A puzzled Frank Dallas was left in his cell while the others were paraded before Judge Samuels in the main building. The judge was feeling rather poorly because of his cold and had a raspy sore throat so that his remarks were hard to hear.

Most of Group A received all-of-life sentences if they had killed – and this included Todd Yancey who had a bandage around his head, covering the wound made by the bullet Dallas had fired at him when he had slashed at Jessica Gowan's throat.

The red-eyed judge stared long and hard at the sick-looking kid. Todd had worked up enough spunk to return the stare with a stubborn tilt of his chin.

'You, Yancey, are a special case – it has been established beyond doubt that you, Zack Ballard and the late, unlamented Mohawk Magee were the ringleaders of this riot and I personally suspect that your father was the one behind it all. You and your cohorts dragged sick women from their beds, killed one nurse, injured two more and attempted to murder Nurse Jessica Gowan. Fortunately, your home-made knife was blunt and she threw up her arm as you attempted to slash her throat. Still, the arm was cut very deeply and she was forced to resign her position here which was her livelihood...'

The judge paused to sneeze and Todd started to say *'Gesundheit!'* but one glare from Samuels and his teeth clicked together. He grinned sourly in token defiance.

'Yancey,' the judge said firmly, straining so that his raspy words could be heard all round the large room, 'you are hereby sentenced to life imprisonment in this penitentiary – with hard labour. I am going to mark your papers *Never to be released.'* Samuels leaned forward quickly and pulled his dry lips back tightly across his teeth.

'You want to grin some more, you murderous little scum?'

It was afternoon before Dallas was taken from his cell, allowed to wash up in the ablutions block and then taken before Judge Samuels. The hearing was in a room at the rear of the main building where a fire burned in a stone fireplace. The judge had a blanket around his shoulders, sitting in a chair in front of the flames, holding a kerchief to his raw, dripping nostrils. Warden Luckett stood to one side while an armed guard stood at attention by the window.

Luckett announced him quietly and Samuels turned his rheumy eyes on to the prisoner.

'As I said earlier, Judge, I'd like to recommend this prisoner for parole.'

Dallas gave a start at the warden's words, looked sharply at Luckett. Samuels was frowning deeply, wiping his nose vigorously.

'On what grounds?'

'On the grounds that he prevented the escape of three prisoners, rescued three hostages and surrendered himself without resistance.'

Warden Luckett went on to explain about Dallas's part in shooting down Mohawk, wounding Zack Ballard and also Todd Yancey.

'I'll be frank, Dallas, and I mean no pun by that – I don't like gunfighters. I particularly don't like you. You have not served the minimum time for parole consideration but, when such time *is* served and parole is petitioned, I will take into account what the warden has just told me...'

'Judge, I really think we could bend the rules a little,' Luckett said firmly. 'Yancey would have killed Nurse Gowan and escaped by boat if Dallas hadn't intervened.'

'How can you be sure he did not intervene simply because *he* wanted to escape? He may have simply taken the opportunity when it arose, wounded Yancey, intending to take his place in the escape plan.'

'No, Judge, I didn't see it that way,' said Luckett.

Samuels held up a hand, sneezed several times, blew his nose and looked exasperated. 'Warden, I am on my way to my sickbed. I do not wish to delay any longer. I will give some thought to what you have told me, but, at present, my decision is that Dallas serve out his full time, or at least the minimum requirement before consideration is given to parole. I am too ill to discuss it further ... call my carriage, please.'

Returning the disappointed Dallas to his cell Luckett said, 'I'm truly sorry, Dallas. It's bad luck that the judge is feeling so poorly.'

'Don't think it made any difference, Warden, but I thank you for trying. How's that nurse? She really give up her job here?'

'No choice. Prisons Department are moving out all female inmates, temporarily at least, and giving all female staff their notice. They don't want a repeat of that riot with women being used as hostages.'

'Can savvy that. They ought to make sure

164

of it and hang that Yancey kid.'

'Well, he'll be in Maximum Security from now on and when Ballard recovers, he'll be there too.'

They had reached Dallas's cell and he nodded wearily, went back inside, not even turning around when the strap-iron door clanged shut with a cold and brutal finality.

Bo Kirby rolled away from the frolicking prostitute and lunged for the six-gun on the chair beside the bed as the door of the room crashed open.

He twisted, the hammer spur coming back under his thumb, the cartridge in the cylinder lining up with the barrel as the Colt swung up and steadied on the intruder. The naked girl screamed and rolled off the bed on the opposite side, thudding to the cold floor.

Solomon Yancey yelled as the gun snapped into line and he never knew how close he came to having his head blown off his shoulders.

Kirby cursed and lowered the hammer swiftly, twisting. 'The *hell* are you doin', Sol?'

Yancey strode around the bed, yanked the frightened girl to her feet by one arm, scooped up her dress where it hung over the end of the bed and flung her unceremoniously out into the hallway.

By the time he turned back, the gunfighter had pulled on a pair of trousers. 'What's happened, Sol?'

'That goddamn judge! He – he...' Yancey seemed to be choking in his anger, unable to spit out the words. 'He's given Todd a life sentence!'

'*Judas!*' Kirby was genuinely shocked. '*Life,* for Chris'sake!'

'*And* he's stamped his papers *Never to be released!*'

Kirby shook his head slowly. 'By God, that's bad news, Sol!'

'*Bad?* It's a goddamn disaster!'

'What's Ball doin' about it?'

'Ah, he's talkin' appeal and all that legal

crap but that'll take months.'

Bo Kirby nodded slowly, looked at his boss with eyes that seemed almost sleepy because they were partly closed. 'Time for my plan?'

Yancey hesitated just a moment, then nodded jerkily. 'Yeah! Time to put your plan into action – right now! I should've listened to you first time round.'

'I been waitin' for your OK!' Kirby said, pulling on his woollen shirt. 'Just waitin'!'

It was cold on the street and there was slush from the last sleet storm that muddied his boots. Kirby swore softly as he dashed across through icy rain, slipped and almost fell on the wet boardwalk opposite. There were few people about in this late afternoon and those that were had their heads buried in hoods or their faces hidden by turned-up collars and no one took any notice of him as he hurried along to the La Grande hotel.

He went down an alleyway and to the outside wooden stairway that led to the upper floor of the town's biggest hotel.

In minutes he was standing inside the door at the top of the stairs, looking at the number on the nearest door. *Eighteen* – he wanted fifteen so crossed the dim hall – the lamps weren't burning yet despite the early gloom – and found the room he wanted. He tapped on the panel with his knuckles.

'Yes?' answered a quiet female voice, and the door opened and he smiled at Judge Samuels' puzzled daughter.

Before she recognized him she said, speaking quietly, 'Please don't make any noise. Baby's not well and I've only just now managed to get him to sleep ... oh!'

She put a hand quickly to her mouth as she recognized Kirby and stepped back involuntarily, starting to close the door. He pushed one shoulder lightly against it and easily forced it open again, smiling all the time as he stepped inside and closed the door behind him, turning the key in the lock.

'Howdy, ma'am ... won't keep you long.'

Warned by some instinct, Valerie Beldon opened her mouth to scream and Kirby's smile widened as he slapped her across the face, the force of the blow knocking her halfway across the room. She cannoned into a small table covered in ornaments and they shattered as they fell to the floor.

The girl sprawled with a half sob of pain as he stepped forward and towered above her. The smile had a cock-eyed kind of pleasure in it as he unhurriedly reached down with his left hand and twisted his fingers in her lush, dark hair.

The guard said nothing as he crashed open the door of Dallas's cell and jerked his head for the prisoner to step out into the passage.

Frank Dallas threw off the thin blanket and shivered as he pulled on the muddied workboots, wrapped the blanket around his shoulders and obeyed.

'What's going on?'

'Warden's office,' growled the guard and Dallas started forward, prodded by the man's carbine.

Dallas was in for even more of a surprise when he was ushered into Luckett's office. The warden dismissed the guard and pulled Dallas across to the fire. Then, in the shadows, the prisoner saw the form of another man hunched down in a large leather chair, wrapped in blankets and an overcoat. The man was wheezing and sniffing and for a moment he thought it was Judge Vernon Samuels...

Then he was sure – it *was* Judge Samuels!

The clock on the wall read 2.17 a.m.

Dallas looked at Luckett who said quietly, 'Judge has something to say to you.'

Samuels turned his face towards Dallas, and the prisoner's frown deepened when he saw the gouged lines and sunken eyes with dark half-circles beneath. The judge sure looked poorly.

'It's only a few days since I refused you parole, Dallas.' Samuels' voice was hoarser than ever, sounded strangled as he fought to breathe through phlegm. 'But I'm now prepared to ... reconsider.'

Dallas could see how hard it was for the man to say this, glanced at Luckett who kept his face carefully blank.

'Several things have happened,' Samuels grated. He blew his nose, took a deep breath, coughed and wheezed. 'My daughter, Valerie, has been ... assaulted, badly beaten. In fact, she is in hospital, recovering.'

'Who the hell would do that?'

'A man named Bo Kirby.'

Dallas stiffened. 'Sheriff Lake got him locked up?'

Samuels shook his head very slightly. 'No – and he won't be going after Kirby. Or anyone else associated with Solomon Yancey.'

'I don't understand, Judge.'

Samuels lifted a hand from the arm of the chair and let it flop back weakly. 'I – I don't eat crow easily, Dallas... As I said, my daughter was attacked, but worse even than that, my grandson was – abducted.'

Frank Dallas stiffened, going very still, stunned by the news, but remained silent, waiting for Samuels to finish.

'We heard nothing for two days. Valerie had been told by Kirby to make sure no one knew the baby had been taken, especially not to call in the sheriff or they would send back one of the boy's ears...' He had to pause and get a hold on himself. 'We sweated out the time and three hours ago, he came to my place and demanded that I sign a release for Todd within the next three days or we'll never see the baby alive again.'

'You going to do it?'

The judge looked suddenly sunken. He cleared his throat. 'I could not in all conscience turn that murderous young swine loose on society! All right, perhaps there is a little bit of a gamble here, but I have three days and – and I'm counting on you to help me.'

'Well, what can I do? I'm still a prisoner here.'

It was an effort for Samuels to say the rest of it.

'I want my grandson back safe and sound – at any cost. Warden Luckett will release you and when you have succeeded, I will sign perfectly legal papers that will give you your freedom. I don't care what you do to Yancey or this Kirby.'

Dallas smiled crookedly. 'Sign the papers first, Judge. I can't guarantee you anything. Except that I'll try.'

'You don't make the deal, Dallas! You do things *my* way or–'

'Judge, I believe Dallas *is* a man of his word,' cut in Luckett. 'You could sign the papers and I'll hold them if you like until we see how things are going to work out.'

Samuels kept shaking his head, stubborn as all get-out.

'Bother you that you have to bend your rules, Judge?' Dallas asked, unable to resist. 'You, upholding the law, going by the book, yet you have to ask for help from a man who's broken that law almost every day of his life for the past thirty years?'

'Yes, damn you, it *does* bother me! I've been pushed into this by law-breakers! Look at you, a cold-blooded killer, but I have to use you...' He paused. 'But I don't care about myself any longer, it's Valerie and young Vernon Junior I care about now. All *right*, Dallas! You win! And *damn* you for making me do it this way! But you just get me back my grandson and I – I'll be eternally grateful.'

Dallas arched his eyebrows and caught the look of surprise on the warden's face at the same time.

By God, the judge was almost human after all!

10

Freedom

The street door of the law office was partly open when Dallas reached it. He stepped swiftly inside and slammed the door shut behind him as a startled Sheriff Lake came up out of his chair, saying, 'What the hell?'

Dallas didn't say a word. He swung a punch that shot out from his right shoulder like a pile-driver and Lake's head snapped back on his shoulders and he staggered and stumbled out of the chair, crashed into the wall and slid down to the floor where he sat blinking, blood dripping from his nose. His eyes were almost crossed and he said and did nothing at all as Dallas reached down for him, dragged him over by the desk, sitting him back against the front of it.

Big Arch's head lolled loosely on his neck as Dallas fumbled at the man's gunbelt, undid it, yanked it free and buckled it about his own waist. He pulled the stag-handled Colt from the leather, examined it and swore softly.

'You lazy son of a bitch! You haven't even oiled it!'

Lake struggled to pull himself upright by the desk and Dallas helped him, sat him down in the chair.

'I want my rifle, too.'

Lake blinked at him, held a handkerchief over his bleeding nose. 'I heard the judge had let you out, but if you think you can come in here and assault me...'

Dallas leaned down, grinning mirthlessly. 'But I can, Arch. I can do just about any damn thing I like in this town and the judge won't lift a finger to stop me. Or help you or anyone else who bitches about my actions.'

The sheriff frowned. 'That ain't so! Judge Samuels would never make a deal like that.'

'He did. You check with him and he'll tell you to co-operate with me ... and what I want first are my guns.' He slapped a hand against the Colt and Lake stiffened. 'How'd you like it, Arch? Feel good to pack a gunfighter's Colt?'

'All right, all right. It just looked a good gun and – well, I figured one day I might be able to sell it, for a decent price. Your rifle's in the cupboard.'

Dallas turned, then heard a sound behind him as the sheriff heaved up out of his chair, swinging a big fist. The gunfighter ducked easily, slammed a blow into Arch Lake's ample midriff and the lawman grunted, sat down heavily in his chair again. By then Dallas had his rifle and levered a shell into the breech, pointing the gun at Arch. The man half-raised his arms protectively across his face.

'What happened to my horse?'

'Judas, man, it's long gone!'

Dallas prodded him with the rifle. 'What *happened* to it, Arch?'

The lawman swallowed. 'It was – sold to the livery.'

'You still have the money?'

'Me? Hey, I din' say *I* sold it! Any money'd belong to the County, anyway.'

'Get it for me, Arch ... now!'

'Son of a bitch!' Arch muttered under his breath but he opened a drawer and took out a battered cashbox.

The livery man tried to act tough until Dallas banged the rifle butt down onto his bare foot and splayed his toes for him. The man howled and hopped around and finally admitted that the buckskin had appealed to him and he had kept it for himself. The horse was in a well-built stable of its own, protected from the cold and with plenty of oats.

He recognized Dallas at once and the gunfighter stroked his muzzle, handed the surly stableman the money Arch Lake had reluctantly given him.

'Hey, what's this! That hoss is worth a lot

more than this pittance.'

'Take it up with the sheriff. He said that's what you paid him for Buck. Now get my saddle and blanket and put them in here – the bridle, too. You look after Buck in this stable until I'm ready to take him. Savvy?'

'It'll cost you–'

'Exactly nothing,' cut in Dallas, eyes boring into the man. 'And he'd better get the best of attention...'

He gave the animal a final pat and then shouldered the stableman aside and went out into the cold of the day.

It felt good to be packing his gun again and to be carrying his rifle. And he was snug and warm in the big leather-wolfskin jacket that Luckett had provided as well as clothes from the prison slopchest. He had managed to get a pair of good-fitting Levis in reasonable condition, good boots only a little tight, and a warm grey woollen shirt.

All in all, he thought, as he walked down the street, watching folk give him strange, wary looks, Frank Dallas was loaded for bear.

All he had to do was find one – *two*: named Solomon Yancey and Bo Kirby.

Sol Yancey looked sour as he confronted Bo Kirby. A part-time whore was doing her best to pacify the crying Baby Beldon in a corner of the rented cabin.

'What the hell's wrong with that kid?' Yancey demanded.

'I dunno,' whined the whore, who was little more than a teenager. 'I dunno nothin' about babies 'cept how to avoid havin' 'em.'

Sol scowled at the gunfighter. 'Get rid of her! That kid's sick – and by Christ, he'd better not die on us!'

'What about my money?' the girl whined.

Kirby tossed a double-eagle into her lap, just missing the crying baby. 'There. Now put the kid down on the bed and git. Sol, we can't take that kid to a doctor. I dunno spit about kids. We need someone who does. The prison got rid of all the nurses when they sent the women to other jails. Must be one or two still hanging around town who need the work.'

Sol heaved a sigh, and nodded, watching as the girl gathered her few pitiful things, hesitated, and wet a finger and placed it briefly on the baby's burning forehead.

''Bye, love. Hope you get better quick.'

Yancey took her by the arm and thrust her out the door, slamming it after her. He glared at Kirby.

'Well, what're you waitin' for? Go find a nurse and some medicine.' He pointed at the howling baby. 'And make it quick! That kid's your responsibility now!'

'Well, thanks a lot, Sol! What am I gonna do? Teach him how to shoot a gun? 'Cause that's all I damn well know!'

'Just hurry up, damn you!'

Muttering, Bo Kirby shrugged into his warm jacket, set his hat, checked that he could reach his gun in a hurry if necessary and stormed out.

Sol was pleasantly surprised when Kirby returned in just over an hour with a brisk-looking young blonde woman who had her left arm heavily bandaged. Kirby introduced Jessica Gowan who nodded to Sol, who Bo said was 'Mr Solomon', set down her grip on the floor and picked up the baby. She spoke to it, making soothing, cooing sounds, unwrapped some of the clothing and shawls. The injured arm didn't appear to hamper her much.

'Too many clothes on him. He has a cold, or the beginnings of one.'

Sol looked at her eagerly. 'He's all right then? He ain't gonna die on us?'

Jessica smiled faintly. 'I shouldn't think so, but this is a draughty cabin...'

'Place is all I could rent in town.'

'Well, you should rent another, a warmer place. I'll need some things at the druggist's, too...'

'Bo'll get whatever you need – and after you bring the stuff back, go hunt up a better place to stay.'

Kirby didn't like being ordered around in front of Jessica but nodded, took some money that Sol handed him and after Jessica told him her requirements, he went out.

'Where's the baby's mother, Mr Solomon?' Jessica asked, as she changed a soiled napkin.

'Unable to care for him. It's – family business. I don't want to discuss it ... you do a good job and I'll pay you well, miss.'

Jessica's hazel eyes stared steadily at him. 'How long do you want me to take care of him?'

'Just for a few days. Now, there are some things I want to get straight. The baby's father is lookin' for him so I don't want you tellin' anyone where he is. Fact, you'd better stay with him full-time until this – trouble is settled.'

She frowned slightly. 'All right. But I may have to get some more clothes for him, if you don't have any spares.'

'We don't. But Bo'll get whatever you need.'

She laughed. 'D'you think Bo would go into the general store, into the women's section, and ask for a baby's bonnet, a dozen more diapers, a feeding bottle, some powdered formula, a pacifier...?'

'All right! All *right!* You can get those things later but just don't say who they're for ... understand?'

'Whatever you say, Mr Solomon.'

Frank Dallas was becoming frustrated.

He felt like he had worn out a pair of boots traipsing around Yuma, trying to get some clue as to where the judge's kidnapped baby may be.

He had prowled the streets looking for Bo Kirby without success, although a couple of times men had told him he had just missed the gunfighter.

He went into a saloon on Gila Street, pushed up to the bar and thumbed back his hat as he signed to the barkeep to bring him a beer.

'Bo Kirby been about?'

The barkeep shook his head, recognizing Dallas now without his moustache and wearing clean clothes. 'Ain't seen him ... but that feller at the end, name of Tyrell, he works for Sol Yancey, too. Might be able to help you.'

Dallas nodded, drank down his beer, took his empty glass and walked down the bar, pushing in beside the rangy cowpoke-type the 'keep had pointed out. Close up, the man looked mean and he slid his gaze sideways at Dallas, stiffened, obviously recognizing the gunfighter.

'Looking for Bo Kirby – but maybe you'll do, Tyrell.'

'Go to hell, Dallas. I want no truck with you. An' don't get the notion it's because I'm scared of you, 'cause I ain't ... could beat you if it come to that.'

'You want to go outside and try?'

Dallas's readiness startled Tyrell. Then he curled a lip. 'You anxious to go back to Yuma?'

Dallas shrugged. 'I won't be going back – cut a deal with the judge.' Deliberately boasting now. 'I can do about what I like in this town.'

Tyrell's jaw sagged open and the men around were listening with their ears hanging out at Dallas's words.

'Hell, I don't believe that!' Tyrell said, and Dallas grinned tightly.

'Mister, you just called me a liar. Now that *is* a shooting matter.'

Tyrell was startled again at Dallas's willingness to drag iron, but he was an arrogant, bullying man and had a lot of faith in his own ability with a gun. 'Well, I ain't backin' down!'

Dallas gestured to the rear door. 'Nice day for it – let's go.'

He started to move away from the bar, but Tyrell hesitated. 'Now, wait up–'

'Backing down?' Dallas was deliberately pushing the man and Tyrell swore, downed the last of his whiskey, made to hitch up his trousers – and instead, slapped a hand against his gunbutt, drawing very fast.

The room shook to the sound of a single shot and men stumbled out of the way as Tyrell was spun back along the bar, his unfired Colt spilling from his hand, his gun-arm shattered at the shoulder by Dallas's bullet. Sobbing, he fell to one knee.

Blood dripped from his fingers as Dallas stepped forward, holstering his gun. He knocked Tyrell's hat off and dragged him out the side door into the alleyway where a cold wind whistled, dumping him in a heap against the clapboard wall.

Someone poked his head out the door and Dallas told him to get the hell out of it. The door closed quickly.

'Tyrell, I know you're hurting like hell so the quicker you answer my questions, the quicker you can go see a sawbones.'

Tyrell spluttered a curse and Dallas rapped his head against the clapboards.

'Where's Sol Yancey? I want to know where he's taken the judge's grandson.'

Tyrell looked a bit afraid now. 'I – I dunno nothin' about that. I'm just s'posed to hang about town in case I'm wanted. Me and some others of Sol's troubleshooters.'

'Like the ones he sent in those boats to

rescue Todd? Yeah, I recognize you now. You were in one boat, lucky to get away. But not so lucky to run into me.'

Tyrell was really feeling the wound and his shattered collarbone now and he moaned. 'I'm speakin' gospel! Get me to a sawbones, Dallas! I – I'm gonna pass out.'

'Not till you tell me something – you know *something* about that baby deal. Now, tell me or you'll have a foot wound to show the sawbones as well.'

He drew his six-gun, cocked it and aimed at one of Tyrell's boots. The man scrabbled to draw his leg under him but the shoulder wound was giving him hell and he said, 'All I know is they hired a – ranch – somewheres north of town. Small place. Been abandoned for a while. That's all I know ... I swear, Dallas!'

'See? Your memory's not as bad as you thought...'

Dallas spun as the saloon door opened and Sheriff Lake stepped out, shotgun in hand, but he didn't lift it when he saw

Dallas holding his Colt.

'The hell you doin'?'

'Talking with my friend Tyrell. He had a little accident, cleaning his gun and it went off or something.'

'Yeah! Or *somethin'!* I been in the bar, I know what happened. So you're in trouble – again.'

'Arch, have you checked with the judge yet?'

The lawman hesitated, then nodded curtly.

'Then you know there's no trouble I can get into in this town that needs you poking your nose in.'

'*Goddamnit*, Dallas! It – it ain't *fair!*'

'Go have a drink on me, Arch. Tell the 'keep I said I'll pay.'

'Now look here! I'm still sheriff...'

'Go have the drink, Arch,' Dallas said firmly, and the sheriff swore bitterly, argued feebly a little longer then suddenly whirled and went back into the saloon. Tyrell was staring wide-eyed at Dallas, his pain

189

forgotten for the moment.

'Judas, I ain't never seen anyone do *that* to Big Arch before!'

'Something to tell your grandkids – if you live that long.' Dallas heaved Tyrell to his feet. 'Somehow I believe you, Ty. I'll help you to the sawbones, but after he patches you up, I'd clear town if I was you. Kirby gets to hear you and me've been talking and he'll come after you to see what you told me ... and he won't believe a thing you say.'

Tyrell swore and nearly fainted as Dallas hauled him along the alley.

Jessica Gowan came out of the general store with her package of items for Baby Beldon, tore open the brown paper wrapping to check that there was a teat attached to the feeding bottle. Satisfied, she started down the street, saw Dallas coming out of the infirmary. At first she wasn't sure it was him and then she was: most of the town knew he was out on parole. But parolees usually weren't allowed to carry guns.

She waved and he shielded his eyes against the sun, then walked across. 'How's the arm?' he greeted.

'Coming along. That prison doctor is hiding his light under a bushel – he's an excellent surgeon. Have you hurt yourself?'

He realized she was asking why he had been in the infirmary. He told her briefly.

'They said in the general store there had been a gunfight – I – didn't connect you with it...' She let the rest trail away awkwardly.

He smiled. 'Kind of keeping in practice is all... Can I carry your parcels?'

She started to hand them over then changed her mind. He looked quizzical. 'Thanks all the same – but I can manage.'

He looked a mite disappointed but nodded. 'Found yourself a job already?'

'Yes – just light work. Caring for a baby, actually.'

His gaze sharpened. 'Kind of *hard* work, isn't it, looking after a baby?'

'It can be ... but this little fellow won't be much bother.'

She juggled the parcels a little. 'I'd better be getting back. He has a cold and I need to give him some medicine.'

'Can I walk with you?'

She paused, sober now. 'I'd rather you didn't. The people I work for – well, they're a little stuffy ... and...' Her words trailed off: she didn't like lying to Dallas but Solomon Yancey had been insistent about keeping their new location secret – frighteningly so. 'You know how it is,' she finished lamely.

He decided to help her out of her awkwardness. 'Sure, I understand.' He touched a hand to his hatbrim. 'We might run into each other again. Hope so, anyway.'

'Yes, it's not that big a town. Enjoy your freedom, Mr Dallas.'

'I aim to...' He nodded and they parted. He went into a store and bought some tobacco, watching her through the dusty display window.

She turned onto a side street that led north...

Dallas hurried to the livery and saddled

192

his buckskin, rode back to the side street and past the houses there and when they dwindled away to open country he sought the shelter of timber. Leaning on the saddlehorn he searched the open dusty road ahead, saw Jessica's figure way up near a rise. She started up over and disappeared from view.

Dallas rode slowly, dismounted well before the rise and went up on foot after ground-hitching the horse in a patch of grass. He carried his rifle, crawled in amongst some rocks and took off his hat before carefully looking below.

There was a gulch and dust was stirring, leaving a yellowish haze. He got to his knees and saw more dust spiralling up from two horses. In a few minutes they came into view: the girl was riding a pinto and alongside was Bo Kirby on his sorrel gelding. Obviously he had 'been sent to meet her and escort her in.

Dallas hesitated, then ran back to the buckskin, slapped the reins free and mounted, putting it over the rise quickly.

There was only dust to follow for a spell and then the country gave way to a series of hills that disappeared into what looked like a large canyon. He hauled rein, watched for a spell and, sure enough, the riders turned into the canyon entrance between low, sloping rock walls.

Dallas touched his heels to the mount's flanks and rode towards the entrance warily, rifle butt on his knee, a cartridge in the breech, his thumb on the hammer.

It was mid-afternoon and the sun was strong. He was sheltered from the wind down here among the hills, but he heard it moaning through the canyon, dismounted at the entrance and hugged the rocks as he made his way in on foot, the horse staying where he had left it with trailing reins.

At the far end of the canyon, 5 or 600 yards away, he saw the ramshackle ranch building, single-storeyed, part weather-worn adobe, part clapboards that were silver-grey from long exposure to the elements. The roof had some shingles missing, but only on the clapboard end of the house. The corrals had been temporarily repaired and held half-a-dozen horses. There was a barn without doors and he saw Jessica and Kirby dismounting and then the gunfighter escorted her towards the house.

On the rickety porch with a sagging awning, a figure rose out of a cane chair and he recognized Solomon Yancey.

There was nothing he could do now in daylight: it was too open between his position and the house itself. He glimpsed a man at a window and reflected light flashed briefly from a rifle barrel.

He had looked carefully when riding in but there were no guards placed at the canyon entrance now. Still, it might – *should* – be a different story come night-time.

Dallas aimed to find out and lost no time in getting out of there.

One thing worried him: how the hell was he going to get a sick baby out of there, past a crew of hard-eyed gunslingers, without it making a sound?

The last thing he wanted was bullets flying around him while he had a baby tucked under one arm.

11

Failure

Only one guard!

Dallas couldn't believe it. He had been crouched among the rocks on the approaches to the canyon's entrance and he had seen only one set of movements, on the right side above the entrance, a man changing position to get comfortable, later lighting a cigarette. *Some guard!*

But try as he might he could not see any other sign of a second guard. Well, it was remote, a good way from town, and probably an unlikely hideout if anyone was thinking along those lines. An abandoned ranch, likely alive with snakes and pack-rats and other vermin that had moved in meantime was not a place anyone would expect a kidnapper to take an eight-month-old ailing baby.

Jessica had obviously been hired and given some sort of cover story to explain away the baby. She must have believed it for she didn't seem to have any idea whose baby it really was.

Dallas had never been one to let the hours go by in procrastination. He figured out the odds as well as he could, and then decided what to do about them. In this case, he had to get in there and up to the ranch house. That meant getting past the guard. So – get rid of the guard first.

It was an awkward and dangerous climb in the dark and he had to ram his rifle through his belt at the back so as to have both hands free as he felt for holds. Riding boots were not meant for rock-climbing, either, and he slipped a couple of times, literally hanging by his fingertips until his scrabbling boots found a fresh hold to support his weight. Then it was climb some more, sweating in his heavy jacket, knowing that same sweat would chill on him like ice once he reached the top and was exposed to the cold night wind.

He hoped that guard hadn't heard his boots scraping when he had slipped. Panting, trying to control his breathing and keep it as quiet as possible, he floundered over the edge and lay there a short time, letting his heart and breathing settle – half-expecting the guard to materialize out of the night and jam a rifle barrel in his ear.

But there was nothing – in fact, he could still see the faint glow of the man's cigarette end in a clump of rocks a few yards ahead. He eased his rifle out and got slowly to his feet.

Or started to.

There was a slight sound to his left and he swivelled his head sharply, only half-way to his feet. He stumbled slightly, grabbed frantically at his gun. Then saw the dark shape coming in swiftly, heaved upright and swung the rifle by the barrel as the man struck at his head. His hat was jerked off as he ducked and his rifle butt caught the man on the elbow. He howled and Dallas rammed his body into the attacker, sending him stumbling back against a rock. The gunfighter brought the rifle around in a short, violent arc and the man grunted, spilling sideways. *There was someone behind him! A* second guard after all!

Dallas spun but not quite fast enough. A gunbutt hit his right shoulder, numbing his arm so that he dropped his rifle, the Winchester clattering as it fell amongst some rocks. Dallas stumbled to one knee and the other man lifted a knee against his jaw and tried to swing his gunbutt again. Dallas lunged forward awkwardly, arms going around the man's legs. He almost brought the guard down, but the man found his footing and Dallas, head ringing, realized he was in a mighty dangerous position – directly beneath the gunbutt as it hissed towards his head.

He almost made it. The six-gun butt bounced off his forehead, tearing open the flesh, filling his left eye with blood and making a flap of skin. Stars and planets whirled in cosmic chaos behind his eyes and then there was another jarring jolt and he spun away into black, empty space.

It was no fun coming round. As he became more and more aware of the pain in his head and the soreness of his shoulder, Dallas figured he would just as soon stay unconscious.

But icy water dashed into his face and he gasped and jerked upright, feeling the ropes about his upper arms and across his thighs binding him to an old straight-back chair whose dried-out joints creaked and rocked in a warped manner as he moved.

'C'mon big man!' a voice growled. 'Let's see how tough you are. Quit playin' possum.'

Bo Kirby. That made him more reluctant than ever to open his eyes but he did so, slowly, the left one sticky and blurred. He was in a room of the old ranch, of course, tied to a chair, two lamps burning, and several people watching him – including a pale, worried-looking Jessica Gowan. She had some bloodstained rags on a small table beside her with a bowl of rust-coloured water and then he felt the tightness of bandages around his head which throbbed like an Indian drum at a ghost dance.

'You may have a little concussion, Mr Dallas,' she said quietly. 'It was a hard blow you took.'

'Never mind that,' growled Kirby, standing over Dallas, putting a hand under the man's jaw and jerking his head back roughly.

Dallas felt sick and stifled a moan, looking up at the grinning gunfighter. 'I'll put your mind at rest for you, Dallas, I ain't gonna kill you. Not yet – I want you alive so you and me can square off.'

Dallas swallowed, his mouth very dry. 'Then you're right – you ain't gonna kill me: I'll kill you.'

He paid for that with an open-handed

smack across the face that turned his head on his shoulders and set his ears ringing even louder. Jessica gasped.

'Stop that! If he has concussion...'

Her words broke off as Kirby slapped her across the face and she staggered into the table, the bowl of water slopping. Her eyes looked afraid of Kirby.

'Go watch the kid,' the man snarled, and Jessica threw a helpless glance at Dallas and went out, rubbing her reddened cheek.

A man heaved out of a chair and Dallas faced Solomon Yancey, as the rancher came over and stood beside him, smoking a cheroot. Sol took it from his mouth, blowing smoke, leaned down.

'Samuels send you?' Dallas said nothing and Yancey, face expressionless, pressed the glowing end of the cheroot against the back of Dallas's left hand.

The gunfighter writhed and bit back gasps of pain. Kirby laughed, so did one of the other men. Yancey straightened, still dead-pan.

'Don't really matter, it has to've been the judge. He let you out yet give my boy life in that hellhole!'

'Should've hung the loco son of a bitch!' Dallas growled, prepared to take the pain he knew must come.

And it did.

It lasted forever, or the longest five minutes of Dallas's life, anyway. When it was over, he hung semiconscious against the ropes, blood dripping into his lap from his mouth and nose, the room spinning around him.

Both Sol Yancey and Bo Kirby were breathing hard, Bo sucking the split knuckles on his gun-hand.

'You did say the judge had sent you, didn't you, big man?'

Dallas set his blurred vision on Kirby, forced himself to grin, blood on his teeth giving him a maniacal look. 'I came to get you, Kirby. Figured it was time someone laid you to rest ... want to cut me loose and we'll have at it?'

Kirby scowled and straightened, but Sol placed a hand on his arm, shaking his head. 'Can't you see he's proddin' you? Now settle down, you'll get your chance at him later. Dallas, this was a bad, *baaaad* move on Samuels' part. But he just don't realize it yet...' He gave his attention to Kirby. 'Bo, keep him here till I get back.'

Kirby looked surprised. 'Where you goin'?'

'To have me a talk with the judge... *Nurse!*' He raised his voice and a few moments later Jessica entered the room, the baby cradled in her arms.

'I've just got him off to sleep. You'll have to keep the noise down.'

'I'll make as much noise as I damn well want!' snapped Sol, but he didn't raise his voice very loud. 'Cut me a lock of the kid's hair.'

The nurse blinked and stared.

'Cut me a lock of the kid's hair!' This time he did raise his voice and the baby jumped, tiny fists waving in the air, face contorting as he

started to cry in fright.

'That was very smart!' Jessica said, rocking the frightened baby gently, turning and leaving the room.

She came back alone, the child still crying in the room behind her. Silently, she handed Yancey a curling lock of golden baby hair. She cast a worried glance at Dallas before she left while Sol carefully placed the hair in a soft leather wallet.

'Bo, you're in charge, but don't you kill Dallas. He might be useful. With any luck, I'll come back with Todd.'

Dallas snapped up his throbbing head. Kirby straightened. The other two men in the room looked at each other at Yancey's words.

'The hell you gonna do?' asked Kirby.

Sol was getting into his warm clothes and merely said, 'Just do it like I said. Mightn't be back before daylight so don't get to worryin'.' He gave a crooked smile. 'I'm holdin' *all* the aces this time.'

He went out and Kirby, annoyed that

Yancey hadn't taken him into his confidence, vented his spleen on the bound Dallas for a few minutes until he tired of hitting an unconscious man.

He wrenched open the door. 'Nurse, you can patch up Dallas if you want. I want him able to feel everything I do to him when I start on him in the mornin'.'

Jessica appeared, looking worried, grimacing when she saw the bloody gunfighter sagging against his ropes.

As she went to get some bandages and what first aid she had, Kirby said to the red-haired man, who had slugged Dallas unconscious on top of the canyon entrance, 'Red, you watch him. Tag can relieve you later.'

Bo punched the unconscious Dallas one more time in the head as he strode by and left the room. One of the other men followed while the redhead, scowling, settled down on a ramshackle chair, folding his arms. The only sign of animation he showed was when Jessica returned and began to work on Dallas's injuries.

He had taken a bad beating. Both eyes were swollen almost closed. A tooth had gone through his lower lip. One ear was torn slightly, his neck was bruised. His body was blue and purple from hammering fists and his nose, if not broken, was at least badly bent.

By the time she was through, the redhead was dozing in his chair and Dallas was stirring slightly. He managed to focus on Jessica and tried to smile, but it hurt too much and turned into a grimace.

'Obliged,' he rasped hoarsely.

She was shaking. 'I've seen worse injuries, but how any man can cold-bloodedly do this...!' She shook her head and Dallas managed a shrug.

'Takes a special kind of man – a mean, ornery bastard,' he slurred.

She nodded, looked around at the redhead who stirred stiffly. She spoke in a whisper. 'If we could get out of here, d'you think you could make it?'

He nodded. 'Figured you didn't know what was going on here.'

'I didn't. But if you're sure you can make it...?'

'I am.'

'Get some sleep now. You can use it. We'll go later when the whole house is sleeping.'

He tried to say something else but she gathered her things and left, the slight sound stirring the redhead who woke, frowning, and glaring at Dallas.

The gunfighter let his head hang, pretending to be asleep. Within minutes, he was no longer pretending.

Judge Vernon Samuels stared solemnly at the curl of golden hair sitting on the table before him. He shuddered as Sol Yancey said, 'Could just as easy have been an ear or a finger.'

Samuels looked up, his face heavy with his cold and the shock of this middle-of-the-night confrontation with the man he hated most on this earth.

'I've done everything you asked,' he said hoarsely, the act of speaking hurting his raw throat.

Sol shook his head. 'No you *ain't!* I din' ask you to send that gunfighter, Dallas, after me, to try and rescue your kid! *My* kid's still in jail! You ain't let him out yet, like I asked!'

The judge was shaken, staring at the lock of hair shimmering in the lamplight. 'These things take time to arrange, and you did give me three days.'

'Now you got three *hours*,' gritted the rancher and Samuels blanched.

'Good God, man, I can't do that!'

'You will – or the next part of your grandson you see *will* be an ear.' Sol leaned forward, the tip of his stiffened forefinger ramming into the desktop as he spoke. 'You make out a paper that turns Todd loose *immediately!* I'm through pussyfootin' around, Samuels! You tried to blind-side me with Dallas and I'm here to tell you he's comin' back fit only to be buried in Boot Hill! Now, you want your *whole* grandson back, you'll have Todd brought here before sunup. If I don't get back to where I'm stayin' by a certain time, you'll never see your grandson again, won't even find a trace of him, will never know what happened to him – or how many pieces are spread around the countryside.'

'For Christ's sake, man, do you have to be so – so – graphic! He's only a little baby, after all.'

'And you love him, just as I love *my son!* I'm not usually such a pitiless bastard, Judge, but don't you try to call my bluff or you'll regret it till the day you die!'

'You're a miserable swine, Yancey! You're not a caring father, you're a hard-headed, sadistic son of a bitch who's determined to get his own way no matter what!'

Sol Yancey smiled thinly. 'Just like you, Judge. Bet you've sent more men to the gallows than I've had hot breakfasts and you ask how *I* can call myself human?' Yancey scowled suddenly. 'The deal's simple: give me Todd and I'll give you your grandson.

Play me false and by God...!'

Samuels wearily lifted up a hand holding his sodden kerchief. 'All right,' he said, his whole bearing displaying his sense of defeat. 'You win!'

The rancher smirked. 'Never any doubt in my mind about it – oh, one more thing, Judge, you might have some idea that you'll be able to set the law or someone after me once you have the baby back.' Sol Yancey shook his head. 'Don't try it. That grandkid of yours will never be safe if you have such notions. Nor will your daughter – and, when you get right down to it, nor will you.'

12

Doomsday

Red was still on duty in the draughty parlour of the old ranch house in the canyon when Jessica returned. She held a cup of coffee and a small plate of cookies, gave the sleepy redhead a quick smile.

'Had to warm the baby's bottle and made some coffee – thought you might like a cup.'

Red came awake, yawning, took it from her, winked and patted her thigh. 'Thanks, Nurse – I'm feelin' kinda poorly. Tag'll be relievin' me soon. You wanna come to my room and check me over?'

Jessica laughed. 'I've the baby to look after!'

'Well, I need babyin', too. Promise you you won't be disappointed!'

The girl's smile was enigmatic, but she didn't agree or refuse. It was good enough for Red and he pursed his lips and smiled to himself as he sipped the coffee and then started in on the cookies.

Jessica knelt beside Dallas, lifted his head and he opened one blackened eye. She had bathed both his eyes with cold cloths earlier and the swelling had gone down considerably.

'How is your vision?' she asked a little anxiously.

'None too good,' he admitted, sensing she was doing more than just talking. 'Everything's blurred.'

'Hmmm. More swollen than I thought. I'll bathe them again with cold cloths ... they should be better in an hour. I have some arnica tincture, too, that may help.'

'This is good coffee. Lots of sugar, just the way I like my women: hot and sweet!' Red chuckled.

Jessica forced a smile. 'I thought you seemed too sleepy to have such thoughts.'

Red laughed. 'Not me. Anyway, the coffee'll wake me up.'

'Don't bet on it,' she whispered near Dallas's ear and he nodded gently to let her know he understood.

It might have worked, except for Tag. The man was unable to sleep and decided to relieve Red on guard duty a little early. He arrived before the drugged coffee had taken effect, although Red was decidedly sleepy.

Tag swore. 'Hell, you could sleep on a barbed wire fence... Go on, git to the garbage heap we're usin' for a room! I'll take over here.'

Red yawned, slurred, 'Thanks, Tag,' and stumbled out. So when Jessica returned, instead of finding Red in a drugged sleep, she found Tag, fully awake and looking into the coffee cup suspiciously. He glanced up as she entered.

'There's white powder in the bottom of the cup! Tastes bitter. Lots of sugar, too, to cover it up ... you been druggin' Red's

215

coffee, you bitch?'

Jessica was taken off-guard, blustered her denial and even to Dallas, it made her sound guilty. Tag jumped out of his chair, swearing.

'Run, Jess!' Dallas called and she started to turn, but Tag grabbed her arm and pulled her back towards him, swinging at her head. He connected and she staggered – and so did he as her full weight dragged at his arm.

Dallas threw himself backwards, hard as he could and, as he had hoped, the old, warped, dried-out chair collapsed. The ropes holding his upper arms against his body fell away and he stepped out of those that had been around his thighs. Tag was almost upon him at this moment and Dallas, still clutching the coarse coils of rope, lashed the man across the face. Tag staggered and dragged at his gun as Dallas threw himself at him, drove him against the wall.

His legs like rubber, he nonetheless hammered blows into the man's midriff, snapped at Jessica, 'Get the baby and go! *Go now, damnit!*'

'But you...'

'*Judas! Get the baby and go!*'

His urgency at last communicated itself to her and she flung herself out of the room just as Tag came around swinging and put Dallas down. The battered gunfighter struggled to get to his feet and a boot slammed into his ribs, sending him skidding halfway across the room. Tag bared his teeth and came after him, stomping.

Dallas put his hands in front of his face, slid on his back across the floor as fast as he could, Tag stalking him and yelling,

'Bo! Slim! Help me!'

That's torn it! Dallas thought, as he rolled painfully to hands and knees and launched himself at Tag's leg. He brought the man down heavily, took a boot on his good ear, then locked his arms about the flailing limb, using it as a lever to half-rise, putting on the pressure. Tag bared his teeth, tried to ease the pain in his hip, and then Dallas stomped on his genitals and Tag gagged sickly and collapsed, just as the door burst open. Bo Kirby entered in his underwear followed by another ranny wearing only a pair of ragged levis and one sock.

Kirby took in the situation at a glance and he and Slim both rushed Dallas who was swaying unsteadily on his feet. He didn't stand a chance against the two of them but he fought wildly and savagely, aiming to keep them occupied for as long as possible so as to give Jessica and the baby every chance to get away.

But it was inevitable that he should go down and stay down, beaten semi-conscious again, swimming in treacle as he tried desperately not to fall off the planet.

Kirby was raging, panting, looking around the room wildly. He dragged the sick Tag over to a chair and slammed him into it roughly. Tag gagged and retched, causing Kirby to leap back.

'The hell happened here?' Kirby demanded, but Tag was still too sick to make any sense – and by that time Kirby was aware that there was the sound of a departing horse coming from up-canyon. He glared at Tag.

'Who the hell's that?' he demanded, and when Tag tried to answer he grew impatient, shouldered the puzzled, half-asleep Slim out of the way and ran to the room where Jessica had been caring for the baby.

His blasphemy echoed through the house when he found the room empty and he raged back into the parlour, glaring at Tag.

'The nurse! Did she take the kid?'

Tag nodded. 'Dr-drugged Red...' he managed, but by that time, Kirby was going out the door, yelling, 'Keep an eye on Dallas till I get back!'

Solomon Yancey jumped out of his chair as the door opened and the man Judge Samuels had despatched to the Yuma jail stood to one side to allow Todd to enter.

'By Christ we did it!' Yancey crowed, striding to throw his arms about his son.

Todd was dressed warmly enough – Sol had insisted on that, too – but the kid had a wild, strange look in his eyes as he said, 'Good to see you, Pop ... where's the judge?'

'He's coming,' said the servant who had shown Todd in and held the door as the judge came in shuffling in his robe and slippers. The servant left silently, closing the door.

Todd laughed – and it had a kind of wild sound to match the look in his eyes. 'Well, well, well, so I get to see you when you don't hold all the aces, eh, Judge?'

'You're free now. Get out of my house. Both of you.'

Sol nodded. 'I've got what I came for. I'll arrange for your grandson to be brought back to you safely.'

'Maybe you'd better stay until that happens,' Samuels said and it was obvious he had collected his wits now and was trying for the upper hand once more.

Todd walked across and threw the judge into a chair that almost overturned. He leaned down and spat in the older man's face.

'Todd!' snapped Sol in alarm, grabbing his son's arm. 'Never mind this! You're free now. Let's get the hell outa here and head home to the Muggyown! That's all that matters – just you an' me, headed for home.'

Todd flung his father's hand off with a savage motion that brought Sol up on his toes. The boy's face was white with a simmering fury, his eyes burning. 'I got scores to settle before I go anywhere!'

'Never mind them, damn you!' Sol shouted, angry now. 'You do like I say! I've busted my ass on this for you, put myself at risk. Now, *let's get out of here!*'

Todd's face straightened a little at his father's tone: after all, he had been used to Sol's authority all his life and so reacted instinctively. But his jaw hardened and he suddenly snatched up the desk lamp with its beaded china shade and smashed it into a corner under the heavy drapes. Hot, blazing oil clung to the fabric and within moments they were afire for their full length. By that time, Todd was laughing as he smashed the other lamp, tossing it through the doorway into the judge's parlour that was expensively furnished.

'*Now* we can go, Pop!' Todd laughed, taking him by the arm. 'But I sure would like to stay... I love a fire! Specially to see a big house like this burning!'

Sol saw it was too late to save the place and bustled Todd out past the judge who was screaming hoarsely for his servants.

In the confusion, before the whole town was wakened by the volunteer fire crew as Judge Samuels' mansion blazed in the night like a massive Roman candle, the Yanceys got clean away.

However, Sheriff Arch Lake did try to stop them. He stepped out of his office, half-dressed, with a gun in his hand and called out to the two riders to haul rein.

Todd reached over, pulled his father's six-gun from his holster and shot the lawman twice, the impact of the lead knocking Big

Arch flat on his back.

'Where you belong, you son of a bitch!' snarled Todd. 'If it hadn't been for you, I wouldn't've been sent to Yuma! *Now* I'm about ready for home, Pop! Let's go!'

The two riders disappeared into the night.

Jessica was afraid she was going to drop the baby as she rode recklessly up the canyon towards the entrance, the chill night wind numbing her face. She clutched the tiny bundle that was Vernon Beldon closer to her body, her heart pounding, as she veered towards the dark entrance.

She cried out aloud in shock as a gun fired twice behind her.

She did not realize it was a warning for the lone guard stationed above the entrance until she turned into it and found a man standing spraddle-legged, pointing a shotgun at her.

She reined down sharply, almost spilling out of the saddle, struggling to protect the now crying baby.

In minutes, Bo Kirby arrived and dragged her out of the saddle, baby and all, and led her back to the house, telling the guard, 'Watch out for Sol just after daylight, Wes. He ought to have Todd with him.'

'Sure hope so. I wanna get back to the Muggyown.'

'Won't be long now.'

In the house, they had Dallas sitting in a rickety chair in the parlour, Slim and the sick-looking Tag guarding him. Red was still snoring in his drugged sleep in a back room.

'Soon as ... I can stand square, Dallas!' gasped Tag, holding his crotch, 'I'm gonna ... kill you!'

'Better not,' Dallas said quietly. 'Kirby's saving me for himself.'

'Hell with Kirby! I–'

Dallas suddenly gave a cry of alarm and threw his arms out as the old chair creaked and swayed and gave way beneath him. Tag stared but Slim started to laugh ... he should have watched like Tag. Only Tag was in no condition to do anything about what he saw.

He saw Dallas grab one of the broken legs as he apparently scrabbled around trying to get on his feet and by the time Tag could yell a warning to Slim, the lean man was writhing on the floor, hands to his bloody face. For good measure, Dallas hit him again.

Then he scooped up the man's six-gun, was surprised to see it was his own. Slim must have taken it when he was first captured. He slammed the barrel across Tag's head as the man fought to get on his feet and the unlucky Tag sighed quietly and folded up in a heap on the floor.

Dallas quickly ripped the gunrig free of Slim's waist and buckled it on. He was still a little groggy, but he figured the cold night air would help bring him around. He found his hat, jammed it on, locked Red in the back room and then went out the sagging rear door as he heard horses at the front.

It wouldn't be the Yanceys back yet but it could be Bo Kirby and – *damn!* – he heard the crying of the baby. The man had caught up with Jessica before she could clear the canyon.

Dallas slid along the adobe part of the house swiftly, reached the corner just as Kirby dismounted and took Jessica by the arm, shaking her.

'Just about your style, Kirby, picking on women and babies!'

Bo Kirby actually jumped at the sound of Dallas's voice, spun about, hand slapping his gunbutt, but not releasing the girl who was struggling to hold the baby.

'By God, Dallas, you got more lives than a cat!'

'Got my own six-gun back off Slim, too. You been bad-mouthing my gun speed for a long time now, Kirby. About time you put up or shut up, ain't it?'

Kirby had the nurse pulled half in front of him and took a snap shot at Dallas. Adobe sprayed as the gunfighter stepped back swiftly.

'Knew you didn't have the guts for a

square off,' Dallas taunted. 'You know you're a dead man if you do call me out.'

Bo Kirby swore. 'I *am* callin' you out! Right *now! Let's see who's got guts or not!*'

'Suits me,' Dallas called, and dived low as he went around the corner, hearing Jessica scream a warning.

'His gun's already out!'

Dallas expected it, rolled as Kirby shot twice and dirt and stones kicked against his body as he twisted around and put three bullets into Bo. Jessica had thrown herself aside when she had called out and Dallas had seen this in the split second before he started rolling in the dust.

Bo Kirby staggered, still tried to wrench his collapsing body around for a final shot. Dallas put him down with a bullet between the eyes...

Jessica fell against the wall, clutching the baby against her, shaking wildly, just managing to stop herself from crying.

'I – I felt the wind of those bullets!' she gasped.

Dallas steadied her, shucked fresh cartridges from the belt loops and began thumbing them into the smoking cylinder.

'We'd better get out of here,' he said, and at the same time heard the sounds of racing hoofs coming across the canyon.

There was lightening grey in the east now, enough to show the canyon entrance, and two dark riders lashing their mounts as they rode in fast.

'The Yanceys!' Dallas said, taking Jessica's arm and pushing her into the house.

A gun roared and a bullet chewed splinters from the door planks. A second gun blasted and two bullets punched through the thin clapboard wall. Dallas kicked the old door closed but it didn't shut firmly in the warped frame. He grabbed the girl and bore her to the floor with the baby.

'Crawl into the other room,' he told her, seeing Tag and Slim were still unconscious. 'I'll see what I can do here.'

'Be careful! They're killers!'

Dallas nodded, ducked as splinters raked

his shoulders from a fusillade of gunfire.

'Bo! Bo!' called Solomon Yancey. 'What in hell's happened here?'

'Bo's dead, Yancey,' called Dallas. 'Your other men are taken care of. Now I'm coming to get you and that loco wolf you call a son!'

Gunfire raked the front of the house and Dallas lay flat, slivers of wood and mis-shapen, ricocheting slugs whining about him.

'Don't worry, Pop, I'll fix the son of a bitch! I owe him from Yuma!'

'Where the hell you goin'? Todd! Todd!'

There was no answer from the kid and Sol put two more slugs into the house out of sheer frustration. He dismounted and crouched by the old stone horse-trough that hadn't held water for years. *What the hell was Todd doing back there?*

He had his answer in a few minutes. He heard the crackling first, then smelled the smoke, then saw the glow of the fire burning in the dry sotol wood, roughly stacked outside for use in starting the cooking fires quickly because of its flammability.

'Todd! You blamed fool!'

'Fool, nothing, old man!' yelled Todd, his voice cracking with excitement now that he had leaping flames to watch as they consumed the tinder-dry clapboard wall of the house. 'You just watch the doors and windows your side. I'll get these on mine!'

'Hell's sake, boy, there's a woman with a baby in there!'

'So? We don't need 'em no more now, do we?'

Solomon Yancey felt the cold goosebumps spread all through his body as if someone was pouring them on him from a bucket.

'*Todd!*' he croaked. 'Don't be loco, boy! This isn't how it was meant to be! Let's get the hell outa here! They can't touch us once we reach the Muggyown!'

'You leave! I'm staying to watch it burn – and I'll shoot anyone who pokes his – or *her* – nose outside!'

Sol couldn't believe this was happening. It

had *never* been this bad before! Todd had always had some kind of control, even at his wildest, in the past. But this...! He sounded – and was acting – as if he was insane.

Plumb loco, as Dallas had said...

Yancey, his old heart pounding, pushed to his feet and ran around the side of the house, throwing up an arm to shield his face from the wall of heat as the fire took hold. How did this get so far out of hand?

Hell, he wasn't a cold-blooded killer! Sure, he'd killed men when he'd had to, but he hadn't meant all that stuff about mutilating the baby! Judas, he wasn't a *fiend!* He just wanted to scare the judge. But he couldn't stand by for *this!*

But how was he going to stop Todd?

Timbers were blazing and falling, shingles were curling up and popping from the roof. *No one was going to get out of there alive!* The kid had killed them all – Dallas, the nurse, the baby, three of his men, men he had ridden with for years...

Todd was jumping up and down, a crazy,

bright-eyed grin contorting his axe-blade face as he watched the house burn. He saw his father coming towards him.

'Hear anyone screaming yet, Pop?'

Sol shook his head as he came and stood beside him watching his performance in the flickering light of the fire. 'This is cold-blooded murder, Todd!'

But Todd didn't even hear him, continued to dance and cheer. 'Aw, son, I never meant it to come to *this!* I – I hope you'll forgive me, boy...'

Sol, tears in his eyes, stepped up behind Todd and clubbed him brutally to the ground with the butt of his six-gun. Todd Yancey didn't move as he sprawled. Sol pulled him back a ways from the fire, ran to the front door, yelling, his voice hoarse with emotion, 'Dallas! Get to the rear door! It's in the adobe section...'

'We already know, Sol.'

Yancey whirled as Dallas and Jessica, shielding the baby from the heat and smoke, came around the adobe part of the burning building. Behind them Tag and Slim staggered under the weight of the still sleeping Red, dropped him on the ground and sat down themselves, coughing, no fight left in them now.

Dallas held his six-gun on Sol, but saw the man had dropped his own gun and was kneeling beside the prone form of Todd. 'I only wanted to get him outa jail an' take him home.'

'What happened to him?' Dallas asked.

Sol looked up, his face contorted, damp with tear tracks through the grime and wrinkles.

'I wish I knew,' he said only half-aloud, and then spoke up. 'Will you give the judge a message from me?' he asked the gun-fighter and Dallas, frowning, nodded. 'Tell him – tell him I said to lock up Todd and to – to throw away the key.' He stood, wiping a hand down his face. 'I don't have a son no more... I'm goin' back to the Muggyown where I belong.'

'You've got crimes to answer for,' Dallas

said and Sol gave him a crooked smile.

'Well, you aim to take me in, you'll have to strap me head down over the back of a hoss. Tag, Slim – bring Red and let's go home, boys...'

He walked away stiffly towards his frightened horse at the front of the house, not looking back, Jessica and Dallas watching him go in silence.

After a moment, Dallas let down the hammer on the six-gun and dropped it back into his holster.

The group stood in the warm sunshine outside the house the judge was renting while his partly burned mansion was rebuilt.

Vernon Samuels' cold wasn't much improved but his temperament was way, way better now as he faced Dallas who still looked battered even though he was cleaned up and dressed in fresh trail clothes.

Jessica stood to one side, cradling the baby who was gurgling away happily, playing with a tassel on his shawl.

'Valerie is improving and will be coming home within the week,' the judge told the gunfighter. 'Sheriff Lake is recovering and has sent men after Solomon Yancey. They'll bring him back. Young Vern is fit and well, I'm pleased to say, and this young woman will have a position here as nurse for as long as she wishes to stay.'

Dallas smiled at Jessica and she smiled back. 'He's a gorgeous baby. I think I'm going to stay for quite a while, Mr Dallas.'

'Frank, Jessica – yeah, it's a good position, better than working in the prison, that's for sure.' He turned to the judge. 'Todd's locked away?'

'Forever, if I have anything to say about it. His father may have second thoughts so I'm preparing to fight a long legal battle, but whatever happens, Todd Yancey needs treatment. He's a mighty sick young man and better off the streets...' He hesitated, looked hard at Dallas, worked his mouth a little and then said gruffly, 'I owe you a debt, I believe, Dallas, for helping save my grandson.'

'You owe me nothing, Judge. I'm free now and that's all I want.' He flicked his gaze to Jessica. 'I'll decide what I'm going to do in the next couple of weeks–'

'No,' cut in the judge and Dallas stiffened, meeting his hard stare. 'No, I'm afraid not. Perhaps you can write and let Jessica know where you end up, but I can't allow a man like you to stay in my town, under any circumstances – you ought to know that.'

'Nice to know a man's efforts are really appreciated, Judge,' Dallas said bitterly.

Samuels stared at him coldly. 'I believe I told you a long time ago, "no exceptions" to my rules. You mentioned going to California once ... why not try it? There's nothing for you here, Dallas.'

'No, I guess not,' the gunfighter said tightly, seeing Jessica's face, as she looked from one man to the other.

Then she smiled. 'Did I tell you I have a sister in Monterey, Frank?'

He smiled back at her. 'Don't believe you did.'

'Oh, yes. We're very close. I'll probably visit her next summer.'

'Hope you do. Good for families to keep in touch.'

'And – friends.'

He nodded. 'Them, too.' He touched a hand to his hatbrim and walked towards his buckskin, swinging up easily into the saddle, then heeled the horse forward and rode away towards the west.

The publishers hope that this book has given you enjoyable reading. Large Print Books are especially designed to be as easy to see and hold as possible. If you wish a complete list of our books please ask at your local library or write directly to:

Dales Large Print Books
Magna House, Long Preston,
Skipton, North Yorkshire.
BD23 4ND

This Large Print Book for the partially sighted, who cannot read normal print, is published under the auspices of

THE ULVERSCROFT FOUNDATION

JUDGEMENT DAY AT YUMA

Gunfighter Frank Dallas only wanted some peace and quiet, somewhere to settle down and hang up his guns after a long life of killing. But the odds were against him and when he shot Harve Lester, he was sentenced to five years in the pen. That was bad enough, but then Todd Yancey showed up, and made the prison tough guys look like fugitives from a Sunday School picnic – and he didn't take to Dallas. By then, Dallas had learned there were only two ways to leave Yuma; either serve your time or die. One day vengeance would be his...